**W9-BIY-741**

When a deadly traitor
threatens to dishonor a top-secret agency,
**A YEAR OF LOVING DANGEROUSLY**
begins....

### Seth Greene
Green eyes, lean muscles—
irresistibly good-looking

*His efforts to single-handedly capture Simon
brought Seth home to the wife he'd left—the child
he had fathered. The family he longed to finally
claim as his own. If only he could...*

### Meghan Greene
A brainy beauty in danger of falling in love with
her ex-husband...

*Because he needed her help, Meghan let the
husband who had broken her heart into her home
once more. Now she wondered if she would be
able to deny anything to the man she'd once given
herself so passionately to....*

### "Simon"
Luck had been on his side so far, but desperation
might be this deadly traitor's undoing....

*With money as his prime motivator,
Simon set about closing a deal that would give
him the cash he needed to complete his evil
mission. Would nothing stop him now?*

Dear Reader,

The year is ending, and as a special holiday gift to you, we're starting off with a 3-in-1 volume that will have you on the edge of your seat. *Special Report,* by Merline Lovelace, Maggie Price and Debra Cowan, features three connected stories about a plane hijacking and the three couples who find love in such decidedly unusual circumstances. Read it—you won't be sorry.

A YEAR OF LOVING DANGEROUSLY continues with Carla Cassidy's *Strangers When We Married,* a reunion romance with an irresistible baby and a couple who, I know you'll agree, truly do belong together. Then spend 36 HOURS with Doreen Roberts and *A Very...Pregnant New Year's.* This is one family feud that's about to end...at the altar!

Virginia Kantra's back with *Mad Dog and Annie,* a book that's every bit as fascinating as its title—which just happens to be one of my all-time favorite titles. I guarantee you'll enjoy reading about this perfect (though they don't know it yet) pair. Linda Randall Wisdom is back with *Mirror, Mirror,* a good twin/bad twin story with some truly unexpected twists—and a fabulous hero. Finally, read about a woman who has *Everything But a Husband* in Karen Templeton's newest—and keep the tissue box nearby, because your emotions will really be engaged.

And, of course, be sure to come back next month for six more of the most exciting romances around—right here in Silhouette Intimate Moments.

Enjoy!

Leslie J. Wainger
Executive Senior Editor

Please address questions and book requests to:
Silhouette Reader Service
U.S.: 3010 Walden Ave., P.O. Box 1325, Buffalo, NY 14269
Canadian: P.O. Box 609, Fort Erie, Ont. L2A 5X3

*Carla Cassidy*

# STRANGERS WHEN
# WE MARRIED

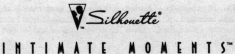

**INTIMATE MOMENTS™**

Published by Silhouette Books

**America's Publisher of Contemporary Romance**

Special thanks and acknowledgment are given to
Carla Cassidy for her contribution to the
A Year of Loving Dangerously series.

To Frank, my own deliciously dangerous hero,
who shares not only my life, but my hopes, my dreams,
my heart, as well.

 SILHOUETTE BOOKS

ISBN 0-373-27116-6

STRANGERS WHEN WE MARRIED

Visit Silhouette at www.eHarlequin.com

**Printed in U.S.A.**

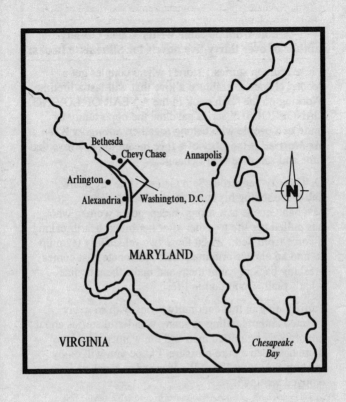

**A note from popular writer Carla Cassidy,
author of over thirty-five novels for Silhouette Books:**

I love reunion stories…stories where couples get a
second chance to embrace a love that will last a lifetime.
Working on the sixth book in the A YEAR OF LOVING
DANGEROUSLY series gave me the opportunity to
unite two people who belong together. *Strangers When
We Married* is the story of a love meant to be, a love that
time and sacrifice won't change.

Deliciously dangerous Seth Greene stole my heart
and made telling his story an absolute delight.
Meghan Greene is a strong, independent woman who
has pulled her life together after her bitter, heartbreaking
divorce from Seth. When these two reluctantly team up
to find an elusive criminal, their passionate past comes
crashing back to haunt them and make them realize
what's really important in life.

Participating in this continuity series with so many
talented authors telling so many wonderful stories about
honorable, committed men and the women who love
them has been a pure pleasure. I hope you will enjoy
reading *Strangers When We Married* as much as I
enjoyed writing it.

Happy reading!

*Carla Cassidy*

# Chapter 1

He dreamed of death and destruction, of guns barking and human carnage. And in his nightmare the dead came back to haunt him, their eyes coldly accusing.

Seth Greene sat straight up in bed, automatically reaching for the gun he wasn't wearing. His heart pumped ferociously, shooting volumes of blood through his veins to his brain, producing the kind of fight-or-flight adrenaline that was intimately familiar.

It took him only a second to leave the dream and gain reality, to remember that he was in the one place on earth he was safe…except from his dreams.

He drew a ragged breath and raked a hand across his jaw, waiting for the burst of explosive adrenaline to subside.

Brilliant moonlight filtered into the large room through the floor-to-ceiling window that provided a spectacular view of the rugged southern California mountains.

He got out of bed and went to the window, hoping the moonlit landscape might erase the lingering vestiges of his nightmares, erase the bitter taste of failure from his mouth.

There were no bad views at the Condor Mountain Resort and Spa. Each window offered a panoramic view of nature at its finest. Towering pines, the Pacific Ocean and rugged landscape gave the impression of a place untouched by man. Even the buildings that comprised the luxury spa were built to blend harmoniously into the landscape.

It had been designed as a place of peace, of healing and tranquillity. But, in the twenty-four hours since his arrival, no peace had entered his soul, no tranquillity had eased the burden of guilt that ripped at his gut.

He turned away from the window and grabbed the jeans he'd kicked off before going to bed. He pulled them on along with a thick, flannel shirt and his shoes, then left the room, knowing further sleep was impossible, at least for the rest of the night.

Unsure of his destination, knowing only the need to escape the confines of the room, he wound down the darkened corridor and found the door that led him out onto the large flagstone terrace.

Once outside, he breathed deeply of the ocean air in an attempt to relax his shoulder muscles that had been knotted for far too long. But, the memory of those dead men, their haunting, accusatory faces in his dream, merely served to further tighten his muscles and sicken his gut.

Back home, it would be cold enough to snow. He tipped his head back and closed his eyes. Washington, D.C., was beautiful in the snow, the stately buildings and picturesque homes with a glistening frosting and dangling shiny icicles.

He frowned and focused his gaze on the sky overhead. D.C. hadn't been his home for a very long time. Almost two years.

The brilliant stars faded as images flashed through his mind, images of a quaint town house in Georgetown, and a woman with eyes the color of a mysterious forest and a mane of curly red hair.

Meghan. He remembered tangling his hands in that glorious hair, kissing sweet, full lips until they were swollen. The memory of their lovemaking was seared into his head. Hot. Hungry.

Swearing beneath his breath, he whirled around and placed his hands on the rough edge of the stone wall, beyond which was a deep, deadly ravine.

"Contemplating jumping?" The deep male voice came from behind him and he turned around to see Easton "East" Kirby eyeing him soberly.

"You know me better than that," Seth scoffed. "I've never been one to take the easy way out." He once again turned to face the ravine. "How did you know I was out here?"

East joined him at the wall. "When you came

down for supper last night, I knew you were coiled too tight to sleep the night through. I've had one ear to the floor for the last couple of hours.''

Seth forced a small smile. "A position like that makes it hard to make love to your wife, doesn't it?''

East laughed, the deep, low chuckle of a contented man. "Don't you worry about Alicia's and my love life. We manage fine, thank you.''

Considering the fact that East's wife, Alicia, was almost five months pregnant, it was obvious they did manage their personal relationship fine, as well as managing the Condor efficiently.

For a moment the two men stood side by side, both of them staring out into the shadowed darkness before them. Around them night creatures rustled in the underbrush, a light ocean breeze stirred the leaves of nearby trees and somewhere in the distance a coyote howled its malcontent.

"I screwed up.'' Seth turned and stared at East's face, focusing on the man's eyes to see if there was any hint of censure there. "I screwed up and a lot of good agents fell.''

He drew a deep, ragged breath as he saw no censure, no judgment in East's eyes, and had instinctively known that he wouldn't.

"Those men knew the risks and if I were you, I'd be hesitant to accept full blame for a blown sting operation.''

"I'm placing blame where it belongs,'' Seth said darkly. "Hell, it's obvious the agency blames me since they sent me here.''

East chuckled once again. "I've never heard anyone before consider coming here as a punishment." His laughter died and Seth felt his gaze on him. "Jonah sent you here because you needed to put things in their proper perspective, because you need to rest and make sure your head is on straight before they send you out again."

"What did Jonah tell you about all this?" Seth's stomach knotted up as he thought of the man he'd give his life for, a man he'd never actually met in person.

Jonah was the head of SPEAR, the covert government agency that gave Seth his orders...the agency that gave Seth a reason for his existence. SPEAR, an acronym that defined all that Seth was as a man. Stealth, Perseverance, Endeavor, Attack and Rescue, an organization to which Seth had pledged his honor, committed his life, and would die for if necessary.

East shrugged his broad shoulders in answer to Seth's question. "You know Jonah...a man of few words. All he said was that the sting was successful in that SPEAR is now in possession of the weapons Simon intended to acquire."

Seth frowned at the name of the man who was attempting to destroy not only Jonah, but the entire SPEAR organization. "Yeah, we got the guns, but Simon escaped...along with seven hundred pounds of uncut heroin." Again a wave of anger and guilt bludgeoned Seth from within. Dammit, it had been his operation. How in the hell had it all fallen apart?

East emitted a low whistle. "Seven hundred... street value will be astronomical."

"Don't remind me."

Again the two men fell silent. Seth stared out into darkness, his mind whirling in chaos. At the same time his mind reeled, he drew in deep breaths in an attempt to give an outward appearance of calm.

"I think maybe I'll do a little hiking in the morning," Seth said, although a trek through nature was the furthest thing from his mind.

East nodded with obvious approval. "Nothing like fresh air and exercise to cleanse the spirit."

Seth forced a yawn. "I'd like to head out at before sunrise, so I guess I'll go back to my room and see if I can catch a couple more winks."

East nodded once again. "Seth, if you need to talk...or anything, you know Alicia and I are available any time."

Seth clapped the tall, powerfully built man on the shoulder. "Thanks, East. I'll be fine." Without waiting for a reply, aware of East's speculative gaze on him, Seth turned and went back the way he had come.

Once inside the privacy of his room, he sat on the edge of the bed, allowing his thoughts full rein. Dead agents...a wealth in dope...and Simon. His mind reeled with frustration, regret and anger.

He remained seated on the bed for a little over an hour, hoping to allow enough time to pass to ensure that East and his wife were sound asleep.

Thankfully, he hadn't unpacked his things the day

before when he'd arrived. The small black bag by the door held everything he needed to live, including two sets of false identification…identification he couldn't use because he didn't want anyone, especially not the superiors who had provided the false credentials, to know where he was going or what he was doing.

He zipped the bag and with the stealth of a wild-cat, opened the door and crept down the hallway in the opposite direction he'd gone earlier.

Not wanting to use the front door in the lobby area, he headed for a little-used service door in the kitchen. He pulled the door open and hesitated in the threshold, torn between duty and desire, following rules or breaking them.

He knew if he walked through the door and into the night, he'd be AWOL. He wasn't sure what repercussions to expect, knew that he'd be considered a renegade agent, but he couldn't worry about that now.

He had to get out of here. Another minute of this peace and tranquillity would kill him. Seth was accustomed to action and he had a definite plan in mind.

Without further hesitation, he stalked out of the door and into the night. The darkness surrounded him, and his dark jeans and shirt camouflaged him as he walked further and further away from the resort.

He needed some answers. Sooner or later Simon would sell the 700 pounds of heroin for cash and more weapons, ammunition he could use to further his destruction of Jonah and SPEAR.

Seth knew only one person who had the sharp intelligence, the innate shrewdness and skilled computer expertise to help him find Simon and the missing drugs.

His ex-wife.

Meghan.

Of course, before he could get her to agree to help him, he'd have to get her to agree to at least see him, talk to him. And that might be far more difficult than finding a cunning, traitorous criminal named Simon.

Meghan Greene believed in the comfort of rituals. She always had a glass of wine before dinner, no matter how long the meal might be postponed.

Despite exhaustion and late hours, she always rubbed hand lotion on her legs and elbows before getting into bed. And every evening before leaving work for the day, she covered her computer monitor with a dustcover and carefully wiped down the glass-topped desk with window cleaner.

This day was no different: She sprayed and swiped, then stepped back to survey the results.

"When you get done over there, how about giving my desk a little spray and elbow grease," Mark Lathrop said as he carried a cup of coffee past her.

"Fat chance," Meghan retorted and eyed his desk with disdain. Discarded take-out food containers littered his space, along with dirty coffee mugs, a plate of three-day-old chocolate éclairs and enough dust to fill a vacuum bag. "It would take more than a little elbow grease on that. You might consider calling HAZMAT to take care of the job."

"Ha ha," Mark replied dryly. He flopped into his chair and eyed her curiously. "Got big plans for the weekend?"

"Sure, me and my best guy are going to spend some quality time together." Meghan swiped the glass a final time then opened the nearby supply closet and put the cleaner away.

"How is Kirk?" Mark asked as he propped his feet up on his desk, narrowly missing the stale éclairs.

Meghan smiled. "He's wonderful." She stole a glimpse at her watch. "And if I don't get out of here, he'll be squalling because dinner is late." She pulled on her coat and picked up her purse.

"Okay, I'll see you tomorrow morning. Turn the sign in the window on your way out."

Meghan nodded and when she got to the door, flipped the sign from open to closed, then stepped out of the front door of the squat redbrick building.

The sign in the front window of the establishment proclaimed it to be the Lathrop Employment Agency, owned by Mark. Although it was true they functioned as an employment agency on the surface, in actuality the office belonged to SPEAR.

The Washington, D.C., traffic was horrendous as usual, and it took Meghan close to thirty minutes to get to the nearby Happy Time Day Care Center.

She hurried to the cheerful room where Kirk spent

his days. "Sorry I'm late," she said to Harriet Winslowe, the white-haired teacher all the children called Grandma Harry. "Hey buddy." She held out her arms as Kirk came toddling toward her, a drooly, happy smile decorating his handsome little face.

"Mama." He grabbed her nose and squealed in delight as she scooped him up and kissed his sweet, chubby neck.

"Was he good?" she asked Harriet.

"Good as gold. I've never seen such a happy baby."

Meghan smiled. "Yes, he is a happy boy." She shifted Kirk from one side to the other. "And growing like a weed."

Harriet smiled. "They tend to do that."

"Yes, they do."

As Meghan bundled the little boy up in his coat and hat, she and Harriet small-talked about the weather and the imminent Christmas holiday.

"Thanks, Harriet," Meghan said when Kirk was ready to go. "We'll see you tomorrow." Within minutes Meghan had Kirk buckled into his car seat and they were heading to the Georgetown town house Meghan called home.

It was a short drive, but as always, by the time Meghan pulled up at the curb in her usual parking space, Kirk was sound asleep. He wouldn't take naps during the day, but each evening on the drive home, he fell asleep and usually napped for a full hour.

After parking, she got out then unbuckled her sleeping child from the back seat. As she picked him up, he curled into her and turned his face into the side of her neck.

Meghan's heart swelled with love. There was nothing quite like the sweet sensation of a child's sleepy breath against your skin.

She took two steps toward her town house, then paused. Frowning, she realized somebody was seated in the chair on her front porch. It was definitely a male. She squinted, wishing she had a free hand to shove her glasses up more firmly on the bridge of her nose. Drat her myopic vision.

At that moment the man stood and instantly recognition flooded Meghan. There was only one man who held himself with such authority that he appeared to command the very air surrounding him.

Seth.

His name exploded in her head at the same time her arms tightened around her son. On the heels of recognition came anger.

What was he doing here? He'd promised... absolutely promised he'd never talk to her, never see her again. He was her past, and that's where he'd promised to stay.

As she walked closer, his features came into sharper focus. She'd never known him when he hadn't needed a haircut, and today was no different. His dark brown hair fell well below the collar of his coat. Despite being unfashionably long and rather shaggy, the style suited his arresting features.

Kirk squirmed, as if protesting in his sleep her tight hold on him. She relaxed her grip a tad, squared her shoulders, then marched ahead, dread rolling in the pit of her stomach.

"Meghan." He nodded his head in greeting.

Before she could reply, her next-door neighbor, Mrs. Columbus, stepped out on her front porch. As usual, the old woman was clad in a duster, this one a swirl of rainbow colors.

"Yoo-hoo, Meghan, dear." The old woman waved and smiled broadly, the gesture causing her plump cheeks to nearly swallow her narrow eyes. "I tried to get your friend to come inside and wait for you where it's warm."

"He isn't a friend," Meghan mumbled beneath her breath. "Thank you, Mrs. Columbus."

The old woman remained standing, as if expecting an introduction to the handsome man on Meghan's porch. But, Meghan had no intention of making one.

Mrs. Columbus stood for a moment longer, her curiosity palpable, then with a disgruntled sigh disappeared back into her house.

Seth hadn't moved during the brief exchange. Meghan walked up the three stairs to her porch and studiously ignored him as she unlocked her front door.

"Meghan, I need to talk to you."

She turned and glared at him. "We had an agreement."

"We did," he concurred. "But my circumstances have changed." His gaze shifted from her to the child in her arms.

"Well, mine haven't." She opened her door and

started to step inside, but he reached out and grabbed her arm, impeding her escape.

"Meghan, it's a matter of life or death." Although his features remained placid and his voice low and calm, she felt the tension that radiated from him.

"If it's your life or death we're talking about, then I'm just not interested," she replied with forced coolness.

"Please." His eyes, those mesmerizing green eyes that had once reminded her of springtime, of burgeoning possibilities and the birth of hopes and dreams, now appeared the turbulent color of stormy seas.

She wanted to tell him no. She wanted to tell him she wasn't interested in anything he had to say. But she'd never before seen him with stress deepening the lines around his eyes, never before felt the kind of desperate energy that flowed from him.

Seth had never needed her before, but as she gazed at him, she felt his need and if she searched deep in her heart she would have to acknowledge that need was provocative.

She sighed and opened her door. "Come in. I'll give you five minutes," she said.

"Thank you," he said simply. He followed her into the hallway and she pointed him to the kitchen. "Sit in there and I'll be right back."

She carried Kirk into the nursery, where dancing bear wallpaper greeted her. Her hands trembled slightly as she placed the sleeping little boy into his crib. He didn't stir as she pulled off his cap and coat, then covered him with a light blanket.

For a moment she remained standing next to the crib, wondering what possible circumstances had brought Seth back into her life. It had been almost two years since he'd walked out, a little over a year ago that she'd contacted him about Kirk's existence and he'd complied by her wishes that he stay out of Kirk's life.

Why was he here? Had he suddenly decided to be a father to his child despite everything? She stared at the little sleeping boy, his brown hair tousled from the hat, his chubby cheeks slightly reddened as they always became when he slept.

"Over my dead body," she whispered fervently. There was no way she was going to let Seth into Kirk's life. There was no way she was going to let Seth break Kirk's heart like he had hers almost two years before.

She'd give him five minutes to explain exactly why he was here, then she'd send him on his way. With that thought in mind, she left Kirk's room and went to the kitchen.

Seth paced the room in restless energy and for a moment didn't see her standing in the doorway. She took that minute to study him, to see what changes had occurred since she'd last seen him.

A little over six feet tall, he still didn't have an ounce of fat on him. His jeans perfectly fit his slender hips and hugged his waist and long legs as if tailor-made. He'd shrugged off his jacket and wore a simple black T-shirt beneath, the short sleeves displaying the taut muscles of his shoulders and arms.

Physically, he looked the very same way he had when they'd said goodbye so long ago. But, something was different and when he saw her and stopped pacing, she realized exactly what was different. His eyes. They'd never looked haunted before.

"You've redecorated," he said, indicating the round wooden table that had replaced the glass-top modern table they'd once owned.

"I needed a change." She walked past him and opened the refrigerator. She took out the leftover tuna casserole and placed it in the oven to reheat. She didn't intend to break her routine just because her ex-husband had shown up out of nowhere.

He paced for a moment longer, then threw himself into a chair at the table and thrummed his fingertips on the tabletop in an irritating rhythm.

Meghan got out a can of corn, opened it and placed it in a saucepan. Placing the pan on one of the stove burners, she looked at Seth. "I gave you five minutes. Two of those minutes have already passed."

He swiped a hand through his hair, looking tense and distracted. "Did you hear about the sting in L.A.?"

"Bits and pieces," she admitted. "You were there?"

He frowned. "It was my baby. I worked closely with Keshon Gray setting up the sting to get Simon."

Meghan moved to sit across from him at the table. "But Simon got away."

Seth nodded. His eyes glittered with hatred for the man who threatened the very foundation of SPEAR, a man they knew nothing about except that he went by the name of Simon. "Yeah, somehow the bastard slipped through. And he took something with him...seven hundred pounds of uncut heroin."

Meghan sucked in a deep breath. "That much smack could finance a lot of trouble."

"Exactly." Again his hand raked through his hair, tumbling the thick long strands into boyish disarray. "That's why I need your help. You can do magic on that computer of yours. You have access to information nobody else does. You can help me find Simon and those drugs."

Suddenly Meghan realized that the moment she'd seen him sitting on her front porch, despite her desire to the contrary, a tiny flare of hope had lit. A hope that he wanted to see her, wanted to be a part of her life, of Kirk's. For a brief few minutes she'd entertained the foolish idea that he needed her as a woman...but what he needed was her as a fellow SPEAR agent.

His words extinguished that tiny flame of hope, and she remembered all the reasons she'd cast him out of her life, out of Kirk's.

"You know I can't do that," she replied curtly. "The kind of information you'd need is highly classified."

"You have clearance," he countered.

"Yes, but if anyone finds out what I'm doing, my clearance could be pulled or I could get fired."

He grinned, that slow, easy smile that had once arrowed straight through her heart. "You're too good to get caught. Besides, it isn't like this would be the first time you've done something like this for me."

She frowned and stared down at the table, knowing what he was talking about. When she'd first met Seth, he'd been assigned to a desk job at the "employment agency" while a leg wound he'd received healed. At that time, Meghan had used her computer and processing information skills to help locate Raymond Purly, the man who'd shot Seth. Raymond had been arrested and was now serving time for the sale of narcotics.

At that time, Meghan had worked beside Seth during the days, and shared a bed with him at night. Their lovemaking had been wild and wicked and wonderful, and Meghan had given him her heart, her soul, and every dream she'd ever nurtured for the future. And he'd taken her heart, her soul, and all of her dreams and shattered them.

"Meghan." Her name was a soft plea falling from his lips, and he reached out and covered her hand with his. "You're the only one I can trust and you're the only one with the expertise to get what I need. Simon is a dangerous loose cannon, and since you're also a SPEAR agent, he's as much a threat to you as he is to anyone."

Meghan yanked her hand from beneath his, hating

the fact that even after all this time his touch still managed to stir something inside her.

She stood, and thought she might hate him…for coming to her at all, for needing her in all the wrong ways. She thought she might hate him most of all for reminding her of the threat Simon posed to the SPEAR agency.

"All right," she said reluctantly. "I can't make any promises, but I'll see what I can find out."

"Great." For the first time since he'd arrived, she saw a slight easing of his tension. "Oh, there's one other small favor I have to ask you."

She frowned irritably, not taken in by the seeming nonchalance of his voice. "What?" she asked flatly.

"I kind of went AWOL from the Condor Mountain Resort last night. You wouldn't mind if I bunked here for a few days, would you?"

At that moment Kirk squalled from his bedroom, a plaintive cry of protest that mirrored the protest Meghan wanted to scream.

# Chapter 2

As Meghan left the kitchen, Seth drew a deep breath and sank down at the table. He hadn't expected the sight of her to affect him, but it had.

The moment she'd gotten out of her car, her red curls bouncing and gleaming in the waning sunlight, his stomach muscles had knotted as memories assailed him. He'd always tangled his hands in her wildly curly hair as they'd made love, loving the way it felt so silky against his fingers.

She'd paled at the sight of him, her freckles appearing to grow darker against the alabaster of her skin. If anyone had told him years ago that at some point in his life an obsessive-compulsive, freckled, red-haired woman would drive him wild, he'd have laughed at them. But that's exactly what had happened.

He and Meghan had shared a crazy, passionate weeklong courtship, then seven months of marriage before reality had intruded and they'd both realized they'd made a terrible mistake.

How many times had he watched those beautiful green eyes of hers darken with desire, light up with laughter, and then at the end of their relationship, cloud with tears?

He shoved back his chair and stood once again, too restless to sit and irritated with the damnable, unwanted memories.

She was a piece of his past and he wasn't here to fix or change the choices they'd made, choices that had led to separate lives for each of them.

Pacing back and forth, he could hear the faint sounds of her talking to Kirk. His son. The boy's little face had been hidden in the curve of Meghan's neck when she'd first arrived.

As he heard Meghan returning to the kitchen, he found himself eager to see the child that he was almost ashamed to admit, until this moment, had been an abstract in his mind.

For the past fourteen months, since the day of Kirk's birth, he'd consciously shoved thoughts of the child away. It had been the only way he could deal with the agreement he'd made with Meghan, the painful agreement to stay out of Kirk's life.

Kirk entered the kitchen first, toddling a bit unsteadily. Automatically, Seth went down on one knee and opened his arms. Kirk stopped at the sight of him. His bottom lip trembled ominously then he turned back toward Meghan.

Meghan scooped him up in her arms and carried him to the nearby high chair where she buckled him in. Seth dropped his hands to his sides and stood once again, oddly disappointed that the little boy hadn't run to his embrace.

You stupid dolt, he told himself. What did you expect? The kid has no idea who you are. Why would he come to you? He doesn't know you're his father. To him you're nothing but a stranger. Nothing but a stranger...and if Meghan had her way, that's what he'd remain.

"Seth, it's just not a good idea for you to stay here," Meghan said. She walked to the refrigerator and pulled out a bottle of wine. She held it up and he shook his head.

As she poured herself a glass, he focused his attention once again on his son.

Seth sat in the chair next to Kirk's high chair. His son. He had his mother's eyes. Brilliant green and at the moment they stared at Seth with both curiosity and wariness. He didn't have Meghan's hair. Kirk's was straight and a dark, rich brown.

My hair, Seth thought, a thrill shooting through him. The child had his hair and his square chin. Kirk had his straight nose and dark brows, yet had Meghan's full lips and cheekbones.

The little boy was an attractive combination of both mother and father and a swell of emotion shot through Seth as he continued to drink in the sight of the little features.

Father. The title rang in his head. I'm his father. For the first time the relationship struck Seth deep in his heart.

"Seth, did you hear me?"

Meghan's voice, tense and with an irritated edge, broke through his reverie. "What?" He tore his gaze from Kirk and focused once again on Meghan.

She handed Kirk a cracker, then joined Seth at the table, her glass of wine in hand. "I said I don't think it's a good idea that you stay here."

"You're right. It probably isn't a good idea," he agreed, then hurriedly added, "but I've got no place else to go."

Her eyes were cold, hard behind her wire-rimmed glasses. "Surely you can think of someplace else."

"If I could, I wouldn't be sitting here right now." He leaned forward and was instantly able to smell her. It was a scent he'd never forgotten, the smell of exotic flowers and mysterious spices. For months after he'd left her, the fragrance had haunted him.

"I need to be someplace where nobody will find me. I need some time to pull myself together, to find Simon. Think about it, Meghan, with the way we parted, nobody would ever think of looking for me here." He smiled dryly. "In fact, this is the last place on earth anyone would look for me."

She frowned and took a sip of her wine. The hard glitter in her eyes had been replaced with uncertainty. She looked at Kirk, then back at Seth.

Seth pressed his case. "Please, Meghan. We're just talking about a couple of days. It shouldn't take you longer than that to find the information I need. I'll sleep on the sofa. You won't even know I'm here."

Kirk banged on his tray, slobbery cracker crumbs decorating his chin. Meghan stared at her son for a long moment, then looked back at Seth. "Three days," she finally said, then downed the last of her wine as if she needed the strength found in the bottom of the glass.

"Thanks," he breathed in relief. He hadn't realized just how important it was to him until this very moment.

"Don't thank me," she snapped. "Understand, Seth, nothing has changed. Our agreement still stands. I don't want you in my life and I certainly don't want you in Kirk's life."

She stood and placed her empty wine glass into the dishwasher.

At that moment the doorbell rang. She whirled around to look at him, her eyes widened in apprehension. "Maybe being here isn't as safe as you thought," she said. "Jonah has ears and eyes everywhere. Maybe they already know you're here."

"Maybe you should answer the door and see who it is," he replied calmly.

He was certain that nobody knew he was here. He hadn't been lying when he'd said the last place anyone from the agency would look for him was here with Meghan. Everyone knew the acrimony that had marked their divorce.

"Yoo-hoo." The feminine voice rang out, followed by a rapid staccato of knocks. "Meghan, dear."

Meghan sighed. "It's my neighbor, Mrs. Columbus."

Seth relaxed as Meghan left the kitchen to answer the door. He smiled at Kirk, fighting the impulse to gather the little boy up in his arms...smell the scent of innocence, feel the cuddly warmth that only a small child possessed.

Kirk gifted him with a shy grin and Seth realized at that moment that he'd made a horrible mistake when he'd agreed to stay out of his son's life.

"I just can't imagine how I managed to run out of sugar," Mrs. Columbus preceded Meghan into the kitchen, her duster swirling around her thick legs and her broad face beaming at Seth. "I like a cup of tea in the evenings, but I can't abide the stuff without a spoonful of sugar."

"It's no problem, Mrs. Columbus," Meghan said as she went to the bright red, apple-shaped canisters on the countertop.

Mrs. Columbus plopped down in the chair next to Seth's. "And there's my little buttercup," she exclaimed to Kirk, who gurgled a greeting in response. "Isn't he just about the sweetest little dumpling you've ever seen?"

Seth grinned. He had a feeling the old woman wasn't here to fawn over Kirk or to borrow sugar.

She was on a fishing expedition. "He is an exceptionally handsome child," Seth agreed.

"We didn't officially introduce ourselves earlier." The woman held out her hand to him. "I'm Rose Columbus, and you're…?"

Seth thought fast. He had a feeling Rose Columbus was not the soul of discretion. He could easily envision her at the butcher shop, haggling over a cut of meat while wagging her tongue over the local gossip. Telling her the truth might jeopardize him. More importantly, telling her the truth might jeopardize Meghan and Kirk.

He took Mrs. Columbus's hand in his. "I'm Steve," he improvised. "Meghan's cousin."

Rose's gray eyebrows danced up in surprise as she looked at Meghan. "You naughty girl, you told me you had no family."

Meghan glared at Seth. "Steve is sort of a black sheep."

"Indeed." Rose returned her gaze to Seth and smiled slyly. "Well, he's a handsome black sheep, if I do say so myself. So, are you staying here long?"

Seth shrugged. "Just for a little while."

"How nice for Meghan to have family over the holidays. Since her scalawag husband left her, she spends far too much time alone," Rose said.

Scalawag husband? What exactly had Meghan told Rose Columbus about him? He raised an eyebrow and looked at Meghan.

Meghan's cheeks were pink as she thrust a plastic bowl of sugar toward Rose. "Here you are, Rose.

That should be enough sugar for several cups of tea.''

''Thanks, dear.'' Reluctantly, Rose stood.

Seth had the feeling she wished she'd asked to borrow something that took a little longer to prepare, giving her more time to pick and prod for information.

''It was nice meeting you, Mrs. Columbus,'' he said.

''Please, call me Rose,'' she replied. ''Perhaps one evening this week you and Meghan and little Kirk can come over to my place and share a little holiday punch.''

''Great,'' Seth agreed easily. ''And Meghan can bring some of her caramel coffee cake. She makes a great coffee cake.'' He studiously kept his gaze away from Meghan, knowing he was probably irritating the hell out of her.

Rose beamed. ''Oh, that would be lovely. I'm quite fond of coffee cake. Well, I guess I'd better get back next door.'' With another broad smile at Seth, she turned and left the kitchen with Meghan following in her wake to show her out.

The moment Meghan left the kitchen, Kirk sent up a wail of displeasure. ''Hey buddy,'' Seth said softly. ''It's all right. She'll be right back.'' He fought the impulse to pick up Kirk, knowing that would probably only make him more afraid.

If nothing else came from this time with Meghan, even if he didn't discover Simon's whereabouts, at least he'd have some time with his son.

And he had a feeling, before his time here was finished, he and Meghan were going to renegotiate their agreement that he stay out of his child's life.

Meghan closed the door behind Rose and drew a deep breath and counted to ten. She was mad...mad at Seth for being here, irritated at him for telling Rose he was her cousin, and especially angry because she felt as if things were spinning out of control.

Hearing Kirk's laughter, she hurried back into the kitchen. She halted in the doorway, stunned by the vision that greeted her.

Seth—the man who'd always exuded a simmering sense of danger, the man who had been trained to deal with criminals and situations that would give most people nightmares—sat with a napkin covering his head and face.

As Meghan watched, he tore the napkin off and grinned at his son. "Peekaboo," he exclaimed. Kirk laughed in delight. Peekaboo was his most favorite game.

Meghan wasn't certain what bothered her more, Kirk's enchanted laughter or the expression of utter devotion on Seth's face. Both filled her with a flutter of fear.

"I'd prefer you don't get him all wound up before dinner," she said as she entered the kitchen.

Seth quickly folded the napkin and placed it on his lap. "I was just trying to make him happy."

"He's a very happy, well-adjusted little boy," she said defensively. She frowned and went to the oven.

"Have you eaten?" she asked as she removed the now-warm tuna casserole.

"Not since this morning," he replied.

Meghan was perversely pleased that all she had to offer him was the casserole, which he'd always professed to hate when they were married. She placed the dish in the center of the table, then glared at him, challenging him to utter a single complaint.

"Hmm, looks good," he replied. The twinkle in his eyes let her know he knew she'd been expecting something different from him.

She handed him two plates and silverware and while he set the table she added the corn, a prepackaged salad mix and dressing, and bread and butter. She quickly microwaved a jar of Kirk's favorite baby food meal…little hot dogs with bits of macaroni, then joined Seth at the table.

They filled their plates in silence, Meghan studiously trying to keep her gaze focused away from Seth. She was chagrined to discover that even after all this time, after all they'd been through, she still found him devastatingly handsome.

"You shouldn't have told Mrs. Columbus you were my cousin," she said, knowing subconsciously she was working up a renewed dose of annoyance with him.

He shrugged. "I couldn't very well tell her the truth. I have the feeling discretion isn't in Rose Columbus's vocabulary."

"I don't like to lie to my neighbors," she returned. "And I suppose you thought that bit about the caramel coffee cake was quite amusing."

He grinned. "Maybe you can fool her like you fooled me...pretend it's homemade when it's actually store-bought."

Meghan frowned, definitely not amused by the memory of the morning after their wedding. Seth had told her his favorite breakfast was homemade, fresh-from-the-oven caramel coffee cake.

Meghan, who couldn't cook at all, had snuck out of bed at the crack of dawn and raced down to a nearby market to buy the treat for her new husband. She would have pulled it off without a hitch had she not forgotten to throw away the box it had come in. Seth had teased her unmercifully.

He picked up a piece of bread and slapped butter on it, then looked at her, one brow raised. "Tell me, what exactly have you told your neighbor about your 'scalawag' husband?"

"Nothing but the truth," she replied evasively.

"Your version of the truth or mine?" he asked dryly.

"What difference does it make? You won't be here long enough for it to matter." She smiled absently at Kirk as he banged on his tray, demanding attention. He wasn't accustomed to sharing his mom.

Despite the fact that Seth had always professed to hate her tuna casserole, he ate like a man starved. He attacked most things with the same single-mindedness.

Even his lovemaking had always been breathtakingly intense. He'd always kissed her like it was a new experience, as if he were starved for the taste of her. Each stroke of his fingers across her body, every exploration of hands and lips had been powerful.

When he'd possessed her, she'd had the feeling he was attempting to brand her, to forever mark her as his, making it impossible for her to be intimate with any other man. And in the darkest hours of the night when she was alone in her bed, she was afraid that was exactly what he had done.

Warmth suffused her and she consciously shoved these thoughts away. The last thing she needed to do was remember their lovemaking. It was the only thing they had managed to do right and it certainly hadn't been enough to sustain a marriage.

"You look good, Meghan," Seth said softly. He pushed his plate aside, his gaze intent on her.

"What did you expect?" she replied, a blush warming her cheeks. "Did you think when you left I'd just fall apart? Fall into a deep depression? Stop showering?"

He smiled curtly and held up his hands in surrender. "Are you this touchy with everyone?"

"No, only with ex-husbands who show up uninvited on my doorstep." Meghan stood and carried her plate to the sink, suddenly weary from the sniping.

She'd agreed to use her expertise to help find Simon's whereabouts and to allow Seth to stay for a few days so there was no use fighting it now.

She turned from the sink in time to see Seth lifting

Kirk from the high chair. The tall man with the haunted eyes held the child a moment longer than necessary, then carefully set him on the floor.

When Seth looked at Meghan, it was impossible for her to read the dark expression in his eyes. All she knew was that at that moment he looked tired… more tired than she'd ever seen him.

"Why don't you go on in the living room and relax," she said. He'd told her he'd left the Condor Mountain Resort last night. He wouldn't have taken a direct route here, which meant he'd had to have traveled for much of the night and day. She knew if he'd been traveling incognito, he'd probably traveled by plane, bus and train to assure nobody could track him.

"I think I will," he agreed.

She breathed a sigh of relief as he left the room. She gave Kirk a plastic set of measuring spoons to play with, then finished cleaning up the counters.

As she worked, her mind whirled with the challenge of finding Simon. She knew the quicker she could accomplish what Seth needed, the sooner he'd leave her home and her life.

When she had the kitchen spotless once again, she scooped up Kirk in her arms and stepped into the living room. Seth was stretched out on the sofa, sound asleep.

For a moment she simply stood there, staring at him as she hadn't dared before when he was awake. She didn't know all the details of the sting in L.A., but even in sleep the failure of that operation showed full on Seth's features.

His long, thick eyelashes rested on dark circles that discolored the skin beneath his eyes. His features, even in rest, appeared taut, as if even sleep couldn't ease the tension within him.

As she watched, his arm jerked, an involuntary twitch that let her know his rest wasn't peaceful. More than ever before, he looked like the man on the edge of both physical and mental exhaustion.

Exactly what had happened during the raid? She knew they'd lost men, knew Simon had escaped, but Seth had been part of unsuccessful operations before. What had been so different about this one? What had caused the haunted darkness she'd seen flash in the depths of his green eyes several times during dinner?

She frowned and hugged Kirk closer to her chest. She didn't care. She refused to care. She couldn't afford to care about Seth ever again.

He'd turned her upside down, twisted her inside out when he'd left her, and she would never, ever give him that power over her again. And she would never allow him to hurt Kirk as he had hurt her.

Shifting Kirk from one hip to the other, she walked down the long hallway to the closet at the end. She grabbed a set of sheets and a thick blanket, then returned to the living room.

Careful not to awaken him, she set the bedding on the arm of the sofa where he would see them when he woke up. If she had a heart, she would have offered him the bed in the spare room instead of the sofa. But having him set up residency in the spare room felt far too permanent.

Besides, she didn't have a heart. Seth had stolen her heart when he'd met her, and he'd broken her heart when he'd left, leaving her nothing but loneliness and broken dreams.

# Chapter 3

Seth awakened just before dawn, surprised to realize he'd slept deeply and without nightmares. The house was dark and silent and cold...especially cold.

In fact, he was freezing. He sat up, stretched, then turned on the lamp next to the sofa. It felt like a meat locker in here.

He grabbed the multicolored afghan from the back of the sofa and wrapped it around him, then reached up and touched the tip of his nose.

Meghan had always liked to turn the furnace way down at night and apparently this peccadillo of hers hadn't changed. His nose felt like an iceberg in the center of his face. He rubbed it several times as he contemplated turning up the thermostat, then dismissed the idea. He was here on shaky ground as it was, no sense pushing his luck.

With the afghan still around his shoulders, he padded into the kitchen and flipped on the small light above the sink.

Coffee was in order, not only to ward off the chill of the house, but to get his brain cells working properly.

He frowned as he pulled the coffee from the cabinet. She'd switched brands. He eyed the container of a gourmet brand he'd never heard of before.

She'd changed the furniture, changed her brand of coffee—what other changes had occurred in his lovely ex-wife?

As he watched the dark brew drip into the glass carafe, he wondered if she still spent long minutes each night creaming her slender, shapely legs before getting into bed? It had been one of those nightly female rituals that had driven him crazy with desire.

He'd lay next to her in bed and watch. He'd smell the heady fragrance of the cream and imagine those long, sweet-scented, silky legs wrapped around him. And when she'd finished, on most nights, his imagination would transform into mind-blowing, sensual reality.

The gurgle of the coffeemaker pulled his thoughts from what had been, and what would never be again. He poured himself a cup of the fresh brew and sank down at the table.

He and Meghan might have remained married forever had they been able to spend every minute of their time in bed. Between the sheets, they had been equal partners, companionable in their wants and needs. Out of bed they had been disastrous.

He'd probably made a mistake in coming here. He wrapped his hands around the mug, grateful for the warmth. It probably would have been better for both of them had he stayed away, had he not seen his son.

Frowning, he took a sip of his coffee.

Kirk.

Seth had never thought much about having children. He'd had Meghan and he'd had his job. He'd believed that had been more than enough to fill his life, fulfill him as a man.

Even when Meghan had called him and told him she was pregnant, the idea of a child had remained vague, a mere abstract in his mind. She'd been so vehement about him staying out of her life, and at the time he'd been so bitter, it had been easy to agree to her terms that he keep away from her and their child.

There had been times in the past fourteen months that Seth had wondered about the boy, but always in his head he'd thought of Kirk as Meghan's child, a tiny entity that had little to do with him.

He recognized now that keeping Kirk a mere abstract in his mind had been a survival instinct. But now the abstract had been transformed into a smiling little face with a mop of dark hair and bright green eyes. Now the abstract had become sweet baby scent and chubby arms and legs.

Suddenly hungry to look at his son, he shoved back from the table and stood. Leaving his half-empty cup of coffee on the table, he walked through the living room and down the long hallway.

The faint illumination of night-lights spilled from each of the doorways in the hall. It had always amused Seth that a woman as bright, as totally together as Meghan, had refused to sleep without a night-light in practically every room of the house.

He had to pass the master bedroom in order to get to the smaller room he assumed to be Kirk's. The third room at the very end of the hall he knew was Meghan's home office, equipped with a state-of-the-art computer system.

Moving with the grace of a cat, he started across the doorway of her room, but paused to peek in before gliding past.

She slept on her stomach, her hair an explosion of scarlet color and wild curls against the pristine white of the pillowcase. The floral bed comforter was bunched at her waist, exposing a soft green night-gown and her freckled shoulders.

He'd once told her that they'd remain married for as long as it took him to kiss every freckle she possessed. And considering the fact that she had a million freckles, the implication was their marriage would last an eternity.

But she'd blown the scenario of eternity. A blast of bitterness laced with pain shot through him. She'd excised him out of her life with a surgeon's precision, with unrealistic expectations and the attempt to force him to deny the very essence of himself.

So much for kissing freckles, he thought as he

moved on past her bedroom doorway. Eventually some other man would have that pleasure and he didn't want to examine why that particular thought bothered him.

He drew a deep breath as he stepped into the small bedroom across the hall, drinking in the scents of sweet innocence and babyhood.

The night-light cast shadows around the room and made the teddy bears on the wallpaper appear almost animated.

The crib was against the far wall, and through the oak bars he could see his son sleeping. Holding his breath, not wanting to awaken the slumbering child, Seth stepped closer...closer still.

Kirk slept on his back and he was snoring faintly. Clad in a dark blue fuzzy sleeper, his cheeks flushed a rosy red, the sight of him expanded Seth's heart.

His child.

His son.

Never again would Kirk be a nebulous abstract in his mind. Seth would never again have the luxury of ignorance, the bliss of not knowing what he was missing.

The desire to pick up Kirk, to hold him tight against his chest was overwhelming. The need to feel the little boy's arms wrap around his neck, feel the snuggle warmth of his body inundated him. Forever now, Kirk would not just be a name in his mind, but rather a face, a spirit, a little person who was a part of Seth.

"What are you doing in here?"

He whirled around to meet Meghan's angry gaze. He reeled at the sight of her. Clad in an emerald green velour robe, with her hair tousled from sleep, she looked as lovely as he'd ever seen her.

She motioned him away from the crib and out of the room. Once they were in the hallway, her expression was anything but lovely. "I don't appreciate you skulking around the house in the middle of the night."

"It's practically morning, and I wasn't skulking around," he protested, keeping his voice low so as not to awaken Kirk. "I...I thought I heard something and just wanted to check to make sure he was okay."

The fabrication tasted vaguely sour in his mouth. She eyed him knowingly and he felt his cheeks warm. He sighed. "I just wanted to look at him for a minute," he finally confessed.

He could tell his answer didn't particularly please her. "It's awfully early in the morning to start off angry," he said. He grinned. "But as I remember, you never were much of a morning person."

"And as I remember, you were always nauseatingly cheerful in the mornings," she replied with a touch of crankiness.

"But I always made the coffee for you," he said, wondering how she could look so damned beautiful with such a scowl on her face. "And this morning isn't any different."

Her scowl eased somewhat and she pulled the robe more tightly around her. "Coffee sounds good," she said grudgingly.

Together they went to the kitchen. She sat at the table while he poured her a cup of coffee and refreshed his own. "What time is it?" she asked.

Seth checked the clock on the oven. "Just a few minutes past six. Did you sleep well?" he asked as he eased down next to her at the table.

"No." She paused long enough to take a sip from her mug. "I didn't sleep well because there was a stranger in the house."

"I'm hardly a stranger. We were married for seven months."

She sipped her coffee, eyeing him over the rim of the mug. Her eyes looked large, luminous, but he knew he was probably nothing more to her than an indistinct shape without her glasses. "Okay," she relented. "We were intimate strangers."

He couldn't argue with that. In truth, it described their brief relationship perfectly. They had been physically intimate, but when they'd finally tried to share their hopes, their dreams, their expectations for their future together, they'd realized their error in judgment about each other.

"What time do you normally go into the office?" he asked.

"Usually, I'm there around eight-thirty or quarter to nine. But, I intend to go in early today and log some time on the computer before anyone else arrives." She frowned thoughtfully. "I can't let anyone know what I'm doing for you."

"Can't you do a lot of the work here? You still have your monster computer, don't you?"

She nodded. "Yes, but I prefer to work at the office. It's less conspicuous for me to use the official computer at work."

Although it sounded logical, he had a feeling she had another reason to prefer working at the office rather than here at home. She didn't want to spend any more time with him that she had to, and she particularly didn't want to give him an opportunity to spend time with Kirk.

Before he left here, he'd make sure he changed her mind about him seeing Kirk. There was no way he could not be a part of his child's life now. But he also knew now wasn't the time to discuss this particular issue with her.

At that moment the object of his thoughts cried out. It was not a cry of distress or fear, rather it was a demand for attention.

Meghan finished the last of her coffee and stood. "Feel free to use the guest bathroom to shower or whatever," she said, then she disappeared out of the kitchen.

Seth got up and poured himself another cup of coffee. He had all day to shower. In fact, he had a feeling the most difficult part of this entire ordeal was going to be sitting in this house doing nothing…waiting for Meghan to come up with the information he needed.

Seth wasn't accustomed to doing nothing. He was a man who thrived on action, craved challenge. Hiding out in a house where nobody was home wasn't very appealing, but at the moment it was his only option.

He walked over to the kitchen window and stared out, watching as the sun crested the horizon, shooting out tentative fingers of light.

It was going to be a beautiful, clear day. It was unusual for D.C. not to have snow by this time of the year. He was grateful there wasn't any. Snow always reminded him of the months he'd spent married to Meghan.

Several weeks of his marriage to Meghan had encompassed the worst winter in D.C. on record, involving blizzard conditions and widespread power outages.

He and Meghan had spent several nights wrapped together in blankets in front of the fireplace, providing warmth for each other. They'd eaten canned pâté and crackers and read to one another by candlelight.

It had been a singular moment, a magical halt of reality when time had seemed to stop and the world outside their home had disappeared.

He turned away from the window in irritation. Damn the memories. They were the one thing he hadn't considered when he'd made the decision to come here. And why such selective memory?

What he had to focus on was the fact that marriage to Meghan had required too high a price…the relinquishing of his very soul.

He turned as she reentered the kitchen, this time dressed for the day and with Kirk in her arms. With her hair neatly tied back at the nape of her neck and the wire-rimmed glasses firmly in place, she looked nothing like the sleepy-eyed seductress she had earlier.

"We're off," she said.

"But what about breakfast?" he asked, his gaze going from her to Kirk, who was clad in a turtleneck and a pair of corduroy overalls. "Even if you don't eat, doesn't he need something?"

"Grandma Harry will give him breakfast," Meghan replied.

Kirk grinned. "Mama Harry," he said.

"Harriet Winslowe at the Happy Time Day Care Center," Meghan explained.

He trailed her from the kitchen to the living room, where she stopped at the hall closet and withdrew her coat and Kirk's.

Seth leaned against the wall and watched as she placed Kirk on the floor and wrestled him into his coat and hat. Kirk laughed, as if it were a game to him, and Seth found a ridiculous grin decorating his own face at the sound of the childish giggles.

"Meghan," he said as she put on her coat and picked Kirk up from the floor. "I know this whole situation is uncomfortable for you, but I do want you to know I appreciate it."

She nodded and ducked her head, as if not wanting him to see whatever expression lit her eyes. "I'm usually home between five and six," she said, then she opened the door and was gone, leaving Seth alone in the cold, empty house.

* * *

Uncomfortable. He'd said he knew the situation was uncomfortable for her. Meghan looked at her wristwatch and stifled a yawn. It was just a few minutes past seven in the morning and already she was exhausted.

She pulled her glasses off and rubbed her eyes. Uncomfortable, that didn't even begin to describe what she felt about Seth hiding out at her place.

He filled the entire house with his presence, invading her personal space with his scent, his very essence. He'd always seemed larger than life to her, more colorful, bolder, stronger than any other man she'd ever known.

Even sleeping, he'd bothered her, making her own sleep elusive. She'd tossed and turned, remembering the look on his face as he'd gazed at Kirk. She'd seen that same troubling expression on his face this morning when she'd walked into Kirk's room and found him standing there.

Shoving the disturbing image aside, she put her glasses back on and eyed her computer screen thoughtfully. If she had a criminal mind and was in possession of seven hundred pounds of uncut heroin, if she wanted to undermine the standing of a secret government agency, where would she go to orchestrate her attack?

The possibilities were endless, the countries who would welcome a traitor and dissident vast. She wasn't sure where to begin a search for the elusive Simon.

As part of her job, Meghan maintained identities

in dozens of chat rooms. Rooms with white supremists, tax evaders, bomb builders and weird splinter religious groups. Meghan knew which groups were truly dangerous and which were merely a bunch of nuts with shared delusions.

But Simon wouldn't show up in a chat room and announce his presence or hold a sale for the drug product. And, of course, it was also possible he'd never left the States and instead was someplace near.

The problem was, Meghan couldn't hunt Simon. She didn't have enough information to track him. She had to hunt down the drugs. It was the only way to get to the man.

For the next hour, Meghan pulled up newspapers from around the country, studying front page stories and crime beat columns to see if any one city was suffering a rise in crimes or deaths affiliated with heroin in the past three days.

The man the SPEAR agents were after had already proved himself more than dangerous. The agency had managed once before the L.A. debacle to intercede a large shipment of weapons intended for Simon. That time Simon had escaped empty-handed. But this time Simon had the means to buy more weapons, and Meghan knew the desire for the weapons and drugs he now possessed were the keys to finding his whereabouts.

There was also one other way to find out what was going on where Simon was concerned, but she didn't want to use that access unless absolutely necessary. She could hack into the most sensitive, secured files in the SPEAR computer, but that avenue was highly risky and she'd only do it as a desperate last resort.

At quarter to eight, Mark breezed into the office, startled to find her already at her desk. "Ah, the early bird gets the worm," he said. "Only in this case it should be the early bird gets the best doughnuts." He placed a box of pastries on her desk as she clicked out of the Montana newspaper she'd been perusing.

"What are you doing here so early?" Mark asked as he took off his coat and hung it on the coat tree just inside the front door.

"I just got around earlier than usual this morning," she said as she scooted her chair to his desk and opened the box of doughnuts. "Hmm, these look wonderful." She grabbed a glazed one as the heavenly scent filled the office.

"It's going to be a slow day," Mark said as he went to the coffeemaker and poured himself a cup of the brew. He then perched on the edge of his desk and grabbed one of the doughnuts from the box. "In fact, it's going to be a slow week with the holidays coming up so fast."

The holidays. Christmas.

Meghan had always hated the holidays…first as a child, then as an adult. And Christmas was the worst holiday of them all.

"I think I'll spend the day putting up decorations outside," Mark said thoughtfully. "I should have done it before now, but I just haven't taken the time. Did you see the display in the window next door?"

Meghan nodded. The dry cleaners who shared the building with them had gone all out. A huge evergreen tree stood in their window, complete with sparkling lights and ornaments consisting of little doll clothes all glittered and sequined in traditional Christmas colors.

"Why bother putting stuff up?" Meghan said between bites. "You'll just have to take it all down again."

"Oh, do I sense a touch of Scrooge in my lovely colleague?" Mark raised a sandy eyebrow teasingly.

Meghan blushed and shrugged. "I just think there's too much holiday hype."

"I adore holiday hype. Have you taken Kirk to see Santa yet?"

"No way. He's too young to be traumatized by a fat guy in a red suit." Meghan popped the last of the doughnut into her mouth and daintily licked sugar from her fingers.

"Definitely a Scrooge," Mark said with a grin.

She laughed and wheeled her chair back in front of her desk and clicked on her in-box, not surprised to find a dozen files waiting for her attention.

As a communications expert, her job entailed analyzing diplomatic communiqués, studying the language used in official speeches and various other materials, then writing detailed reports on what was said and what she believed was meant. Often the two were very different.

Mark finished his doughnut, then disappeared into the large storage closet. He returned carrying a large box filled with glittering garland, plastic evergreen boughs and giant candy canes. "I'll be outside playing one of Santa's elves if you need me," he said.

A moment later Meghan once again found herself alone in the office. As much as she wanted to find the information Seth sought and get him out of her house, she knew she didn't dare spend any more time on his problem right now. She needed to get to her own work so as not to rouse suspicion.

She worked for the next four hours, breaking only to refill her coffee mug and occasionally stand to stretch her muscles. Mark spent the time outside, wrestling with a ladder as he hung lights, garland and giant candy canes from the top of the building.

The door flew open just before noon and a delivery man walked in. He wore an apron that advertised Ling Choo Chinese Cuisine and carried a bag containing a half-dozen take-out cartons.

Mark must have ordered in, Meghan thought in delight. She pulled out her wallet, but the man waved it away, declaring it had already been taken care of.

When the delivery man left, she opened the cartons to find all her favorites...sweet and sour chicken, won ton soup and crab rangoon. There was also chicken chow mein, which she knew was Mark's favorite.

"Hey, Chinese...great idea," Mark said as he came in, his cheeks ruddy from the cold.

"What do you mean? I thought you ordered it," she replied.

"Not me…you didn't?" Mark took off his coat and pulled his chair over next to hers.

She shook her head and frowned. "It must be a mistake. The delivery man must have gone to the wrong office or something. We'd better call them."

"Let's not be hasty," Mark said as he peered at the contents of the cartons. "Odd, isn't it? Everything you like is here and everything I like is here. Was there anything else in the bag?"

"Just a couple of loose fortune cookies." Meghan retrieved the plastic bag the food had arrived in. "Surely you don't think…" She pulled out the two fortune cookies and looked at Mark expectantly.

Mark grinned and shook his head ruefully. "He's been wily before. It wouldn't be the first time he's contacted us through take-out food."

Meghan knew exactly who Mark was talking about. Jonah. Their elusive boss who seemed to be everywhere and nowhere. Mark grabbed one of the fortune cookies, cracked it open and withdrew the fortune.

"Good fortune will smile on you. Lucky numbers are three, five and seven." He looked up and smiled at Meghan. "Maybe I should buy a lottery ticket on the way home tonight."

Meghan broke her cookie apart and pulled out the fortune. "A package has gone missing from the eagle's nest. If contact is made, notify me." It was signed with a familiar J. Meghan's heart quickened.

Mark frowned. "What does that mean?"

"Seth." She wondered if Mark could hear her

heart thundering in her chest. It pounded so hard he must hear it. "He's talking about Seth, who disappeared from the Condor two nights ago."

Mark's brows rose. "He did? How do you know about that?"

Meghan forced a dry smile. "I'm a communications expert, Mark. I know lots of things."

To her relief, he seemed to accept her explanation at its face value. He picked up a set of chopsticks and grabbed the carton of chow mein. "I don't think anyone has to worry about Seth contacting you. Not only do I remember the crime of the century, but I also remember your and Seth's parting as the divorce of the century."

"Please, don't remind me." Meghan set the note aside and tried to keep the nervous tremble of her hand under control.

"I wish somebody would send me to the Condor for about a month of rest and relaxation." Mark stuck a mouthful of chow mein into his mouth. "I guess Seth isn't into vacations."

"I'm sure Jonah is just checking with all of Seth's past acquaintances within the organization." At least that's what she hoped.

She drew in a deep breath to steady herself. She didn't like subterfuge of any kind. Damn Seth for getting her involved in this.

Still, she'd been with the agency long enough to know that this note from Jonah indicated a low-priority concern. If Jonah was truly troubled by Seth's defection from the resort, he wouldn't be contacting people with notes in food that could be easily tossed away. She would have received a phone call from the man himself.

She relaxed somewhat, certain that Jonah had no idea Seth was presently hiding out in her home. But the note from Jonah filled her with apprehension.

She had to find what Seth needed as quickly as possible. The last thing she'd want to happen was to lose her job because she'd chosen loyalty for a man she'd once believed she'd loved over loyalty to SPEAR.

She'd already lost enough to Seth…. She was determined not to lose anything else because of him.

*Chapter 4*

Seth stirred the pot of spaghetti sauce that bubbled on the stove, hoping Meghan would be home from work any time. It had been a lousy day. He'd paced the confines of the house like a prisoner in a jail cell, his thoughts his only companion. And his thoughts were not particularly pleasant.

The faces of the men who'd died in the L.A. sting operation haunted him. The scent of smoke and gunfire lingered in his head, and in that memory, another memory shoved through. It was the distant echo of a tragedy from years before...memories he'd consciously shoved away for almost half his life.

He realized that since the sting, it was as much his distant past haunting him as the more recent catastrophe and he didn't know why.

He'd spent part of the day in Kirk's room, running his hand over the blankets that covered his son at night, touching the toys and stuffed animals that were neatly lined up on the shelves of a colorful bookcase.

Maybe Meghan was right. Maybe the best thing he could do for his son was stay out of his life. Who needed a father who was plagued by visions of death, who spent his time dealing with criminal minds and activity? What kind of a father would he be?

His thoughts would carry him down that path, then go full circle and once again he would find himself vowing to be a part of Kirk's life, telling himself that every little boy needed his father. But no matter how many times he told himself he would be a good father, the doubts returned, niggling in the back of his mind.

He'd finally decided to make dinner, grateful for any activity that momentarily took possession of his mind, keeping troubling thoughts away.

A salad was made and waiting in the refrigerator, the pasta had been boiled—all he needed was for Meghan and Kirk to get home.

He sat at the table, wondering if she'd managed to discover any information for him today. If anyone could pick up signs of Simon's whereabouts, Meghan could do it. She was incredibly bright and superior at her job.

He stood as he heard the sound of a key turning in the lock. He left the kitchen and met Meghan in the entry hall. Her cheeks were flushed a charming pink from the cold and like the day before, Kirk was snuggled against her chest sound asleep.

"You want me to take him for you?" he offered.

"No. I can handle him," she replied. She moved past him down the hallway to the nursery.

She didn't even want him putting the kid to bed. He hadn't returned here to become a parent, so why was that so much on his mind?

She reappeared a moment later and shrugged out of her coat.

"Here, I'll take it." She'd give him her coat, but didn't trust him with his son, he thought as he hung her garment in the hall closet.

"Something smells good," she said as they walked to the kitchen.

"Spaghetti sauce." He gestured her into a chair at the table, then went to the refrigerator and withdrew a bottle of wine.

He knew her routine, knew she wouldn't eat a bite until she had a glass of wine and unwound a little. He poured them each a glass, then joined her at the table. "Does Kirk always nap at this time?"

She nodded and took a sip of her wine. He heard the clunk of shoes beneath the table and knew she'd kicked off her heels. "Almost every evening the ride home in the car lulls him to sleep." She paused a moment to take another drink of her wine, then continued. "When he was just a couple months old he had colic, and the only way I could get him to sleep was to drive around and around the block."

For the first time Seth wondered how difficult it

had been for her so far as a single parent. Had there been nights she'd wished for a companion, somebody to help ease the burden or simply to hold her after a long night with the baby?

Seth got up to stir the sauce, uncomfortable with the direction of his thoughts.

"So, other than cooking dinner, how did you spend your time today?" she asked.

"I watched all the soaps, then went through all your dresser drawers." He laughed as she nearly spit a mouthful of wine. "Just kidding."

The doorbell rang and Meghan's smile faded into a frown of worry. "I wonder who that could be?" She jumped up and hurried from the kitchen.

She returned a moment later carrying a gorgeous Christmas flower arrangement. Bright scarlet poinsettias were offset by miniature red and gold drums and a big gold bow.

"That's pretty," he said, wondering why she carried it as if it were a ticking time bomb.

She nodded absently and set it on the table. Biting her bottom lip she withdrew the small card from its envelope. As she read, the wrinkle across her forehead disappeared and her lips curved up in a smile. "Oh, thank goodness. I thought it might be another note from Jonah."

"Another note?"

She placed the card back in the envelope and tucked it back into the arrangement, then sat once again at the table. "Today in my lunch I found a note from Jonah saying that the package had disappeared from the eagle's nest." The wrinkle returned to her forehead. "You think we should be worried?"

"Nah, if Jonah knew I was here, I'd have already heard from him. I think he was just giving you a heads up."

She nodded. "That's sort of what I thought."

Seth looked at the arrangement. "So, who sent the flowers?"

"A friend." She picked up her wineglass and took another sip, offering no further information.

Male friend or female friend? Seth wondered. Somehow he was certain it had to be a male. Women rarely sent other women flowers.

Maybe Meghan hadn't shouldered the burden of Kirk alone. Perhaps she'd had a companion to emotionally support her. Once again, the thought of her having another man in her life bothered him.

A wail came from Kirk's bedroom. Meghan quickly finished the last of her wine. "I'll be right back," she said.

"I'll get dinner on the table," Seth replied. He moved the arrangement to the counter, his fingers itching to pull the card from the envelope.

It's none of your business, he told himself as he pulled the salad out of the refrigerator and placed it on the table. There's nothing worse than a snoop, he thought as he turned off the burner beneath the sauce.

Of course, if she really hadn't wanted him to look at the card, she would have tucked it into her purse, or carried it with her when she left the room. As it was, she'd left it like an invitation.

He snatched the card from the envelope and read it. *Thanks for the wonderful, home-cooked meal and a lovely evening of fabulous company.* It was signed simply David.

Home-cooked meal? Meghan didn't know how to cook. In all the time he'd been with her, he didn't think she'd ever served him anything that hadn't come from a can or a box.

As he heard her coming back down the hall, he quickly returned the card to where it had been and went back to the stove.

Kirk smiled at him from the safety of his mother's arms. Meghan carried him to his high chair and buckled him in.

"Hey, buddy," Seth said as he added the sauce to the spaghetti noodles. "You ready to try some of your old man's gourmet spaghetti?"

Kirk banged on his tray as if to say, "bring it on."

"He can eat some spaghetti, can't he?" Seth asked.

"If it's cut up in small enough pieces," she replied. "What can I do to help?"

"You can get out the salad dressing and butter," he said as he placed the bowl of spaghetti on the table.

"You know, you don't have to cook for me," she said as she got out the items then sat down next to Kirk's high chair.

"I figure it's the least I can do for all you're doing for me." He joined her at the table. She handed him her plate and he served her the pasta. "I assume if you'd discovered anything for me today you would have told me the moment you walked in."

She eyed him dryly. "Before my coat came off."

"Are you that anxious to get rid of me?" he teased.

"The sooner, the better," she replied, not looking at him but rather focusing on cutting some of the spaghetti into tiny pieces.

She finally looked up at him, her cheeks stained with a faint blush. "It's not every day I have my ex-husband as a houseguest. It's uncomfortable, and if you don't feel that, then you're as insensitive as I remember you being."

"Whoa!" He held up his hands in mock surrender. "Let's not discuss my failings as a husband over dinner. I'll get indigestion."

She smiled, a glimmer of humor lighting her eyes. "Besides, it would have to be a ten-course meal if we were going to discuss all your failings."

Seth laughed and for the next few minutes they concentrated on eating. He watched in fascination as she alternated between feeding herself and feeding Kirk.

Kirk was a demanding little diner, banging on his tray when Meghan didn't attend to him quickly enough. Seth and Meghan laughed as Kirk attempted to use his tongue to retrieve a noodle that had fallen to his chin.

The shared laughter, the utter joy of watching his son, created a bittersweet regret in Seth. For just a moment, he felt the warmth of family. He instantly shoved the uncomfortable emotion aside. How could he regret what had never been?

What he and Meghan had shared had been seven months of a fantasy based on intense lust and good times, but when they'd climbed out of bed and the laughter had stopped, they had been two people with diametrically opposite ideas of what sacrifices marriage would entail. And for Seth, the sacrifice she'd requested of him had been far too high to pay.

"How's Mark?" he asked. "Does his desk still look like the remains of a natural disaster?" They'd finished eating and were clearing the table. Kirk was on the floor playing with an empty egg carton.

"Worse." Meghan laughed. "I swear he has food in his desk drawers that has been in there since World War Two." She took a plate from Seth, rinsed it and put it in the dishwasher. "He spent most of the day today pretending to be one of Santa's elves and hanging garish decorations all over the front of the office."

"Speaking of garish decorations, why don't you have a tree up?" He handed her the last plate.

"I've never really gotten into the whole Christmas thing," she said.

He gazed at her in disbelief. "I seem to remember a certain woman wearing a candy cane-striped teddy decorating a tree while dancing to the tune of 'Rockin' Around The Christmas Tree.'"

To his delight, her cheeks flamed as red as her hair. "I only did that for your benefit, because you were such a sentimental fool about Christmas," she answered softly.

The confession, so unexpected, touched him. Her eyes behind her glasses were the soft green of spring's promise and there was nothing he wanted to do more than take her in his arms and kiss her, transform that spring into summer heat.

"Who's David?" The question came from him unbidden.

The softness in her eyes transformed to something hard and glittering. "You read my card," she said, the accusation laced with anger.

He didn't reply. After all, the answer was obvious. "You fixed him a home-cooked meal? How did you manage that? You can't cook." Someplace in the back of his mind he knew what he was doing... picking a fight to override his momentary desire to kiss her.

"I took a cooking class," she snapped as she dried her hands on a towel. "And I cook very well for the people I choose to cook for."

She bent down and scooped Kirk up in her arms. "You had no business looking at that card, Seth. You're here as a guest and I don't owe you any explanation about the things I do or the people I see. You lost the right to ask me questions when you walked out on me."

"I didn't walk out, I was pushed out," he retorted.

"Whatever," she said wearily. "The point is it's done and past and you have no right to question me about David or anything else. Now, I'm going to work in my office for a little while and see if I can't find you the information you need.''

So you can get out of my life for good. She didn't say the words, but Seth heard them as she left the kitchen.

Seth knew she was right. He'd been wrong to read the card. He'd known it was wrong when he'd done it, and he deserved her anger.

It wasn't until he poured himself a cup of coffee and sat down in the living room that he realized she hadn't told what he'd wanted to know.

Who in the hell was David?

As Meghan waited for her computer to boot up, she arranged a variety of toys around Kirk on the floor near the desk.

She occasionally worked in the evenings at the computer, and Kirk was as at home on the floor in her office as he was in his own room.

He busied himself with a set of blocks, and Meghan slid into her chair and stared at the monitor, her thoughts tumbling like wet clothes in a hot dryer.

She hadn't wanted to remember the one Christmas she'd spent with Seth. It had been a magical time. Seth had been imbued with the holiday spirit and it had been infectious. They'd decorated the house from top to bottom, watched every sappy Christmas movie that was on television, and made love by the base of the huge tree with twinkling lights of red and green.

For the first time in her life, she'd found the joy

in the season. But by the time the season was over, Seth had been gone and she'd realized Christmas, and vows of love, and the concept of forever had all been nothing more than a tinsel-wrapped mirage.

She frowned and typed in her password to access the tremendous power of the computer. She couldn't believe he'd had the audacity to read the card that had come with the arrangement.

She'd met David Prath in the cooking class she'd taken a month ago. He was a nice man, a divorced accountant who she'd shared coffee with twice after class. Last week she'd had him over for dinner, a celebration of completing the cooking course.

There were no sparks with David, nothing closely resembling what she'd once felt for Seth. Although she had a feeling she produced a few sparks in David. Nevertheless, she'd enjoyed spending time together with him and the friendship she felt they were building between them.

She focused on the screen before her. She had to find the information that would get Seth out of her house. His presence was evoking too many memories…painful memories she didn't want to entertain.

Within minutes she'd shoved aside all thoughts of Seth and the past and was fully engrossed in her search for information. Occasionally she would glance down at Kirk, who played quietly with his toys.

She didn't know how long she worked when she checked on Kirk and found him sound asleep, his thumb planted firmly in his mouth. She shoved away from the desk and stood. Stretching with arms over-head, she tried to work out the kinks that inflicted pain in her shoulders.

"Sweet baby boy," she murmured as she scooped up Kirk in her arms. He was such a good boy, such a happy child. She carried him into his room and into his bed. Being careful not to awaken him, she changed his diaper, put him into his pajamas, then covered him with a blanket.

She stood for a long moment at the side of the crib watching him sleep. He doesn't need a father, she told herself. Lots of little boys grew up fatherless. He's happy…well-adjusted and Seth would only be a complication he didn't need in his life.

As she walked from Kirk's room back to her office, she could hear the sound of the television playing in the living room. She could easily imagine Seth sprawled on the sofa, his broad shoulders against the beige material, perhaps one of her burgundy throw pillows hugged to his chest.

She shook her head to dispel the image and once again immersed herself in her computer search. She didn't look up until the door to her office creaked open.

"Are you going to work all night?" Seth asked.

"What time is it?" she asked. She pulled off her glasses and set them on her desk.

"Almost eleven," he replied.

"I didn't realize it had gotten so late." She scrunched her shoulders and rolled her head, attempt-ing to release tension.

Seth stepped up behind her and put his hands on her shoulders. Gently, he began to massage her stiff muscles. "You always did have crummy posture when you work."

"Hmm." She closed her eyes and dropped her head forward, allowing his fingers to dance their magic up her shoulders and to the base of her skull. "You always did give great massages," she murmured as the tension and stiffness seemed to melt away beneath his touch. She breathed in deeply, then released all her muscles and began to relax.

"I used to love giving you those full-body massages," he replied, his voice slightly husky.

Fire licked through her veins as she remembered him pouring scented oil onto her bare skin, his fingers fevered with heat as he worked the oil over every inch of her body.

She stood abruptly and stepped away from his touch. "It's late. Kirk will be up early in the morning."

"Why don't you come into the living room and relax for a few minutes before calling it a night," he suggested. "I made some hot chocolate."

She nodded, suddenly too off center to realize tomorrow was her day off and she wouldn't have the office to escape to. As she followed him from the office to the living room, her neck and shoulders still tingled from his touch. She was going to be cooped up in this house for the entire weekend with Seth. She could feel the tension creeping back into her muscles.

The television was off, the room silent. She sat on one end of the sofa while he went into the kitchen for the hot chocolate. His scent was in air, the evocative male and spicy cologne scent that had lingered in her head for months after their divorce.

She'd been devastated when he'd left, had felt lost and more alone than ever in her life. The discovery of her pregnancy had pulled her from the bleak depression, given her something to love once again.

He returned, carrying two cups and saucers. He handed her one and a reluctant smile curved her lips as she spied the five miniature marshmallows on the saucer next to the cup. He'd remembered.

He caught the smile. "Not four...not six, always five marshmallows," he said as he sat down next to her.

She dropped one into the dark, rich liquid. "Maybe it's too soon," she said thoughtfully, then took a sip of her drink.

"Too soon?" He looked at her blankly.

"For me to find something on Simon. It's only been a couple of days since the sting operation. Maybe he hasn't settled in any one place yet. Maybe he's still in transit and hasn't tried to unload the drugs yet."

"Maybe," he answered. He stared into his cup and Meghan saw the dark shadows that moved to usurp the green of his eyes.

"You want to talk about it?" she asked softly.

He looked up at her, for a moment his eyes mirroring internal torture. "No. There's nothing more to say."

She dropped a second marshmallow into her cup and sipped once again, the silence of the room oppressive. She'd always sensed demons inside of Seth, but the demons seemed to have grown stronger since last time she'd seen him.

"Tell me about Kirk," he said suddenly.

She eyed him in surprise. "What do you want to know?"

He shrugged. "Was he an easy pregnancy? An easy birth?" He set his cup and saucer on the coffee table and leaned toward her. "When did he first smile? When did he take his first step?"

Hunger radiated from him, the hunger to know… the hunger to love his son. The intensity that shone from his eyes frightened Meghan. "It's late," she protested. "Can't we talk about Kirk tomorrow?"

He reached out and placed a hand on her arm. Her body instantly reacted as if he'd stroked her breast or kissed the back of her neck. Heat sizzled through her, tightening the tips of her breasts and creating a ball of tension in the pit of her stomach.

"Please, Meghan. Give me just a little bit. Besides," he smiled, but the gesture didn't quite alleviate the darkness of his eyes, "you can't go to bed yet. You still have three marshmallows left." He removed his hand from her arm.

"It was a difficult pregnancy," she said, feeling as if she were exposing pieces of herself to a stranger. She set her hot chocolate on the coffee table. "I had morning sickness for almost the entire nine months and for the last three of those months I don't think Kirk stopped moving for a moment."

"Did you crave pickles and ice cream?"

She smiled. "No. Pepperoni pizza. I ate so many it's amazing Kirk doesn't speak with an Italian accent."

Seth laughed, the darkness in his eyes ebbing. "And what about the birth?" he asked.

"Fast…as if he couldn't wait to begin his life separate from me." She smiled, remembering the early dawn that Kirk had made his appearance. "He was born squalling at the top of his lungs. No newborn mewling from our son."

Our son. The words hung in the air as if suspended by sheer emotion. Meghan instantly wanted to recall them. She didn't want to give Seth any kind of ownership over Kirk.

"It's late. I've got to get some sleep." She stood and reached for her cup.

"Leave it. I'll get it," he said and also rose. "Meghan." He shoved his hands in his pockets, suddenly looking achingly vulnerable. "Thanks."

She nodded, turned and raced for the privacy of her room. She could handle Seth when he was teasing, or impatient. She could deal with his anger or his laughter, but she had no defenses against his unfamiliar vulnerability.

For the first time since Kirk's birth, Meghan wondered if perhaps she'd made a mistake in demanding that Seth stay out of Kirk's life.

## Chapter 5

"Seth, Kirk is only fourteen months old. He won't know the difference," Meghan protested.

"How do you know that?" Seth got up from the kitchen table and poured himself another cup of coffee.

It was a few minutes after ten in the morning. Kirk had slept unusually late, apparently fooled by the gray, overcast weather that prevented any morning sun from appearing in his window.

They'd just finished eating breakfast and were lingering over coffee when Seth had started the insane discussion.

Meghan fought her irritation, unsure if it was the topic of conversation that irritated her or Seth's appearance.

His hair was still damp from the shower she'd heard him taking before she'd gotten out of bed. Barefoot, and wearing only a pair of worn jeans that rode low on his slim hips, he looked utterly at ease and overwhelmingly masculine.

He rejoined her at the table, his expression sober. "Seriously, how do you know this won't have some sort of long-term psychological effect on him?"

She tugged her glasses off, hoping his bare, broad chest would turn into a simple fuzzy blur. "Seth, we're talking about a Christmas tree here...not hardly the stuff psychoses are made of."

Seth leaned forward, bringing with him the scent of clean, freshly showered male. Meghan wanted to scream at him to put on a shirt, stop looking so good, quit smelling so wonderful.

"I can see it now," he said, his green eyes primal forests with depths to plunder. "Fifteen years from now he'll be on the Montel Williams show, talking about how messed up he is because his mother and father didn't get a Christmas tree for him when he was fourteen months old."

Meghan threw her hands up in surrender. "All right, you win. I'll buy a tree today," she said in defeat. She got up from the table, needing some distance from him.

She rinsed her coffee cup and placed it in the dishwasher, then took a minute to wipe down the countertop.

Ever since last night when he'd reminded her of

those decadent full-body massages he used to give her, she'd felt off center.

She'd tossed and turned in bed, remembering the feel of his hands on her, the hot trail of his lips lingering across her naked flesh. Then she'd thought of the way he'd looked, so proud, so awed, yet so vulnerable, when she'd told him about her pregnancy and Kirk's birth, and her head had spun with confusion.

And then she'd remembered all the reasons she'd asked Seth to stay out of Kirk's life in the first place. Good reasons. Valid reasons.

Despite the softness on Seth's features when she'd talked about Kirk's birth, nothing had changed. She refused to give her son the kind of childhood she'd had. It was best for Kirk if Seth stayed out of their lives permanently.

"Do you intend to wipe the tile clean off?" he asked.

She flushed and threw the sponge in the sink. "I'm going to get dressed and go get a tree." She walked over to Kirk's high chair, unbuckled him and picked him up.

"Why don't you leave him here? I can watch him while you get a tree," Seth suggested.

"No." She tightened her grip on her son and Kirk grunted in protest. "No, I'll take him with me. I have some other errands to run as well and he's used to going where I go."

Seth's jaw muscles tensed, but he merely nodded. Meghan breathed a sigh of relief, grabbed her glasses from the table and quickly escaped to the privacy of her bedroom. At least here, she didn't have to look at his gorgeous bare chest, nor could she smell the scent that was so achingly familiar.

As she dressed, Kirk crawled around on the floor, finally settling on the throw rug and playing with the fringe border.

Standing before her dresser mirror, she brushed her hair. Brush paused in midair, Meghan had a sudden vision of her mother sitting in front of a Christmas tree, a frown of distress creasing her forehead as she worried a damp handkerchief between her fingers.

Instead of Christmas carols playing on the radio, the sounds of a police band filled the house, bringing with it the madness of the season for the cops on the beat.

Armed robbery…purse snatching…shots fired… each crackling call brought tears to her mother's eyes and terror to Meghan's heart.

Would Daddy come home tonight? Daddy, with his blue uniform and shiny badge? Or would something bad happen to him? Would he be taken away from them by a bad person committing a crime?

"All it takes is one nut," her mother would say every night when her father was on duty. "Just one crazy and your daddy is gone forever."

The fear hadn't been contained just to the Christmas season. Every time Officer Robert Roth left for duty, Meghan and her mother feared for his safety.

A childhood stolen in fear.

Seth had the same kind of job…one fraught with danger. Meghan couldn't let Kirk experience the same kind of childhood she'd had. Better to not have a father at all than to entertain the dark, horrible thoughts she'd harbored as a child.

It wasn't as if she'd asked Seth to do something impossible. All she'd asked of him was that he change jobs. And he hadn't loved her enough to do that.

Dressed and ready for her outing, she picked up Kirk and carried him to his room. After changing his diaper and redressing him in extra-warm clothing, she carried him back to the living room where Seth was seated on the sofa.

He stood and approached her as she went to the coat closet. "Let me help you." He held out his arms toward Kirk, who eyed him soberly for a long moment, then leaned forward for him.

Reluctantly, Meghan allowed Kirk to go into his father's arms. As she pulled their coats from the hall closet, she tried not to notice the way Seth held Kirk close to his heart, how he smelled Kirk's hair like a mother dog checking one of its own. She tried not to see how Seth closed his eyes, as if momentarily overwhelmed by holding his son in his arms.

She pulled her coat on, placed Kirk's on him, then took Kirk back into her own embrace. "We'll probably be gone for several hours," she said.

She needed time away from him, away from his irresistible presence. She needed time to steady herself, to get control of the wayward emotions that raged inside her.

"Do you want me to do something about lunch?" he asked.

"No, we'll just grab something while we're out." Murmuring a quick goodbye, Meghan stepped out into the cold, cloudy late morning air.

The smell of snow was in the air. Meghan breathed deeply, effectively banishing any lingering scent reminiscent of Seth. She had to forget how deeply, how profoundly she'd loved him and focus instead on the fact that he'd loved his job more than her.

She shopped for nearly two hours, deciding not only to buy a tree but new decorations as well. Kirk was at the age where he was into everything, so she bought several packages of plastic ornaments just perfect for little chubby hands.

As she shopped, she tried to justify her incredible awareness of Seth. Was it really so strange that he would affect her on such a visceral level?

It had been over two years since Meghan had felt a man's touch, shared a heated kiss. She and Seth had enjoyed a mutually satisfying, lustful, physical relationship during the brief span of their marriage.

Was it any wonder that seeing him again, spending time with him again stirred her on an intense, hormonal level?

But, no matter how much Seth made her remember those passion-filled moments they'd shared over an intense seven months together, there was no going back.

They'd had their chance to grasp happiness, but he'd been too stubborn, too selfish to make the change that would assure them a forever together.

By the time she returned back to the house, the clouds had begun to spit snow and she felt more in control of herself, her emotions. She carried Kirk and her packages into the house.

Seth was in the living room. He'd moved a chair from the corner and the tree stand stood in its place. Lights were strung out across the floor, as if he'd been testing them to make sure none were burned out.

"I see you found the Christmas stuff," she said as she set down both Kirk and her packages.

"Yeah, up in the attic. Some of the lights don't work anymore, but I think I found enough to do the job just fine." His eyes sparkled with boyish enthusiasm. "I hope you got a good tree."

She was grateful that he'd pulled on a long-sleeved flannel shirt, hiding his impossibly broad, hard-muscled chest from her view.

She smiled, finding his high spirits and enthusiasm contagious. "It's not huge, but it's pretty."

"I'll go get it." He started for the door.

"Wait." She grabbed him by the sleeve. "I'll get it. You shouldn't be seen outside."

He hesitated, his brow wrinkling with a frown. "I hate this hiding out."

"But you'd hate the alternative even more." They both knew the alternative was that Jonah would send

Seth back to the Condor Mountain Resort and he would have no opportunity to hunt down Simon.

"I'll be right back," she said. Before he could voice any argument, she slid out of the door and back outside.

It took only a few minutes for her to maneuver the five-foot tree from the top of her car. Seth met her at the door and took over, easily carrying the fat, full tree to the awaiting stand in the corner.

"It's a beauty," he said as he carefully centered it in the stand.

Meghan shrugged out of her coat, noticing that Seth had removed Kirk's outerwear while she'd been getting the tree.

The little boy sat on the floor with the package of the new ornaments in his hands, obviously fascinated by the colorful decorations.

"It's a perfect day to do the tree." He pointed to the nearby window, where the view was of fat, fluffy snowflakes swirling in the air. "Before we start on the tree, why don't I make a fire?"

"Fine with me," she agreed. "The firewood is stacked on the back porch."

"While you were out, your neighbor stopped by," he said a few minutes later as he stacked the wood and kindling in the fireplace.

"Mrs. Columbus?"

"Yeah. She invited us over for cookies and punch tomorrow evening. I accepted her invite."

"You shouldn't have," Meghan replied. "She's

sweet, but she's a busybody. She won't be happy until she knows every detail of your life.''

He laughed. ''I think I can handle one old busybody. Besides, I think she's lonely. It wouldn't hurt us to spend one evening with her.'' He sat back on his haunches and lit the kindling.

Meghan tried not to notice how appealing he looked, with the flames of the fire warming his features. The fire was a mistake, she thought.

With the snow falling outside, the fire in the fireplace and the tree awaiting decoration, the whole scene looked like a picture on a postcard. A happy family preparing for the holidays.

But we aren't a happy family, Meghan reminded herself firmly. We'll never be a family. Seth had seen to that when he'd refused the one request she had of him.

''Okay,'' he said. He stood and rubbed his hands together. ''We'll start with the lights. You want to grab the end of that string?''

Before doing as he asked, she opened the container of the plastic ornaments for Kirk, then grabbed the end of one of the strings of lights.

''We're going to make this tree our masterpiece,'' Seth said, his voice filled with high spirits.

''If you intend to use all those strings of lights, it will be more than a masterpiece, it will be a fire hazard,'' Meghan replied dryly.

Seth laughed. ''Ah, spoken like a true grinch.'' As he reached for another string of lights, he chucked

Kirk beneath the chin. "Did you know your mama was a grinch?"

Kirk giggled, as if he found Seth and his words hysterically funny. Kirk was warming to Seth. Kirk, who rarely took up with men, seemed to find his father quite acceptable.

Not for the first time since Seth's arrival, Meghan felt the need to hurry...to find the information Seth needed so she could send him on his way...away from them. It was what was best. She had to get him away from Kirk.

As she and Seth strung the lights through the boughs of the sweet-smelling pine tree, their shoulders bumped, their hands touched and their hips met as they worked.

Meghan desperately tried to ignore the inadvertent touching, although she warmed and her body tingled at each point of contact.

Did he feel the same? He didn't act like it. He appeared to be completely involved in transforming an ordinary pine tree into a work of art. As their hips bumped once again, Meghan realized she didn't need him out of their lives just for Kirk's sake, but for her own as well.

With the lights all strung, Seth turned them on and stepped back to survey the result. He hadn't realized how dark and dreary the room had become until the tree lit up, illuminating the corner with a kaleidoscope of color.

Kirk laughed in delight and clapped his hands together and even Meghan managed to utter a soft sigh of appreciation.

"While I get the garland on, why don't you find us some Christmas music on the stereo?" he suggested.

She frowned, but moved to the stereo and flipped through the channels until she came to a station playing holiday music.

As Seth strung the gold garland around the tree, Meghan went into the kitchen to fix a cup of juice for Kirk. When she returned and Kirk was happily drinking from the lidded cup, Seth handed her a box of ornaments.

For a few minutes they worked together, hanging ornaments on the tree branches. The music created a soothing ambiance but Seth was anything but soothed.

Meghan smelled too good. Her long, curly hair taunted him, glittering magically in the multicolored light show that spilled from the tree.

He didn't want to hang ornaments. He'd much rather tangle his fingers in her hair, pull her mouth to his and kiss her until they were both breathless. Instead of trying to decide where would be best to display the miniature Santas and snowmen amid the limbs, he'd rather have the dilemma of deciding which of her freckles to kiss first.

Who would be helping her decorate the tree next year? Would there be a man in her life to help her pick out a tree, help her carry it in and get it centered? Would there be a man who would help her tuck Kirk into bed, then take Meghan into her room and kiss the freckles that so taunted Seth?

Would the man be the David that had sent the arrangement to her? Would he not only be Meghan's significant other, but also stepfather to Kirk?

"So, tell me why you hate Christmas," he said, needing conversation to keep his thoughts out of dangerous territory.

She frowned, her eyes somber behind the wire-rimmed glasses. "I don't hate Christmas exactly," she said thoughtfully. Her fingers played over the surface of a glittery miniature sled. She had long, slender fingers, the nails painted a pearl pink.

Seth focused on the tree. He'd always found her hands incredibly sexy. "Were you traumatized by Santa when you were little? Did one of Santa's elves goose you?"

She laughed, a spontaneous sound as pleasant as the music that surrounded them. "No. I wasn't goosed by an elf, nor was I traumatized by Santa." She hung the sled on a branch, the laughter fading. "You know my father was a cop."

He nodded. "A good cop from everything I've heard." Although she'd rarely spoken of her family, the few times she had it had been with enormous affection, especially for her father.

She sank down on the sofa, pulled her glasses off and set them on the coffee table. "He was a good cop, and he was a wonderful father until the day he died."

Her voice held a wealth of emotion. Seth knew

how hard she'd taken her father's death and that the pain of her bereavement was with her still.

"Meghan, what does your father have to do with Christmas?" he asked softly. He knew her father hadn't died around the holidays. The old man had passed away in his sleep on May 10, four years before.

He started to join her on the sofa, then realized Kirk had fallen sound asleep on the floor, the juice glass empty beside him.

He pulled the afghan off the back of the sofa, covered the sleeping child, then sat next to Meghan and looked at her expectantly.

Her cheeks flushed with color. "It's silly, really," she began, looking down at her hands clasped tightly together in her lap. "My father was committed to the job. He'd work whatever shift, whatever holiday they needed him to, but for some reason the nights around the Christmas holiday were the most difficult for my mother."

"Why?" Seth realized that for the seven months they'd been married they'd rarely spoken in any great depth of their families or their pasts. It had been as if they'd both been born on the day they had met, with no past...no future separate from each other.

"Mom said Christmas, like a full moon, brought out all the crazies, so we'd worry more about Dad during that time."

"And all that worry was for nothing," he replied. "He didn't die on the job."

"That's true. We worried for nothing." She slid a

strand of her shiny hair behind her ear, her frown deepening. "And it's more than that. Christmas has gotten crazy. People buy gifts for others not because they want to, but because they feel obligated. Parents go nuts trying to find the toy their child can't live without." She shrugged, then gazed at him. "What about you? Do you have good memories of Christmases past?"

Her question took him by surprise. "Sure, I've got terrific memories." The lie tasted bitter in his mouth. He stood and grabbed another box of ornaments, needing some sort of physical activity to keep the personal demons that had awakened at her question at bay. "Come on, we'd better get this finished up while Kirk is sleeping. Otherwise, we might have more help than we really need."

She got up and once again joined him by the tree. He handed her one of the ornaments, then took one for himself. "You know, it's funny. During all the months we were married, you never talked much about your family."

What was funny was that she'd come to the same realization he had only a few minutes earlier. "There isn't much to say."

Despite his easy, laid-back tone, tension tightened his stomach muscles. He hung another bauble on the tree. "I told you when we first met that my father died when I was seventeen, my mother when I was twenty, both in car accidents."

Somewhere in the back of his mind, he was amazed that his voice could sound so cool, so utterly unemotional as he spoke the lie he'd lived since the day of his seventeenth birthday.

She reached for another ornament. "It must have been so hard...losing your parents so close together when you were so young."

He shrugged. "You get through what fate throws at you."

"Don't you find it strange that we were married and we never talked about stuff like this?" Her expression was serious, her eyes so soft, so inviting. "We never talked about our childhood or our parents, didn't discuss the good and bad things that happened to us that made us who we are."

He took the ornament from her hand and hung it on the tree, then turned back to her. He reached out and trailed a finger down the side of her cheek, across her full lips.

Her mouth pursed slightly as if in response to his touch and the tiny action stirred a fire inside him.

"You know me, Meghan." He leaned toward her, so close his head filled with the scent of her and he could see the tiny flecks of gold that merely served to intensify the green of her eyes. "Talking was never my strong suit. I much prefer action."

She stepped back, away from his touch and he dropped his hand to his side. "Maybe that was our problem, Seth." Color jumped into her cheeks and she averted her gaze from his. "We spent too much time in action and not enough time talking."

He took a step toward her and once again touched the smooth skin of her cheek. "Regrets, Meghan?"

Her gaze met his and in the green depths he saw strength. "I can't regret our relationship. Without it I wouldn't have Kirk."

"And our divorce?" He wasn't sure why, but his breath suddenly felt as if it was an unwilling captive of his chest.

"No regrets, Seth." Her voice held a ring of conviction. "No regrets about that, either."

"Good," he nodded. "At least we're in agreement about that." As he turned his attention back to the tree, he frowned, wondering why he felt as if he'd just told a lie.

# Chapter 6

They finished with the tree about four, joined by Kirk who woke up in time to help with the final touches. After they were finished, Meghan took Kirk and disappeared into the kitchen to make something for dinner and Seth paced the living room, feeling edgy and irritated and unsure why.

Meghan's brief questions about his past had stirred sleeping dragons, evoking memories he'd prefer to forget...thought he had forgotten.

When he'd told her he had pleasant memories of Christmas past, it hadn't exactly been a lie, but it hadn't exactly been the whole truth, either.

Christmas was generally the one time a year his father rallied from his deep depression. He'd indulge in a few drinks and with the spirit of the alcohol flowing through him, he'd spin yarns about the days when he'd been an FBI agent.

His eyes would shine with a momentary flicker of life, and in those old stories, Seth found his own love for the law. He'd just become an FBI agent when the SPEAR agency had recruited him. And within the first few days of working for SPEAR, Seth had realized he'd found his home, the place where he belonged.

And it was the one thing Meghan had wanted him to give up, the one thing she'd wanted to take away from him. He hadn't understood her wish then, and didn't understand it now. She couldn't have loved him…not really…and asked him to give up his work.

He shoved his memories aside and grabbed the fire poker. He stirred the dying embers, then added several more logs. It was uncomplicated to stir the embers of a near-dead fire, far more complicated to stir the dead embers of a relationship.

And why on earth would he want to stir anything up between himself and Meghan? Nothing had changed between them. The issue that had forced them apart still stood between them, would always stand between them no matter how deeply they cared about one another.

Besides, he was better alone, he told himself. Better to move fast and unencumbered through life. That way you couldn't disappoint anyone, couldn't let anyone down. You served only yourself and in the end only had to face yourself.

"Seth?"

He turned from the fireplace. "Yeah?"

"You ready for some dinner?"

He nodded and followed her into the kitchen. Kirk was already in his high chair and he greeted Seth with a happy grin.

Seth tried to ignore the way Kirk's smile seemed to be able to slice through any defenses he had and attack him in the softest part of his center.

"It smells good," he said as he sat at the table.

"It's nothing fancy...just hamburger casserole and a salad." As she set the food on the table, he noticed she appeared subdued, and he wondered what was going on in her head.

Although her features were expressive, he'd never been able to read her thoughts. It was one of the things he'd always found fascinating about her...the fact that he couldn't begin to guess what she was thinking at any given moment.

They ate in relative silence, the only sound Kirk who chattered between bites. It was as if he were showing off, saying all the words he knew and waiting for praise from the two adults.

"Bite," he said and picked up a piece of the hamburger meat. He popped the meat into his mouth, then pointed to his eye. "Eye," he exclaimed, then smiled as if enormously pleased with himself.

"You've done a good job with him," Seth said.

Her eyes lit with surprise. "Thank you. He's a good boy."

"Goo boy," Kirk echoed and smiled broadly.

"He must get his intelligence from you," Seth observed with a small smile.

He was grateful to see her return the smile. "Oh, I don't know. You're not too short in the intelligence department."

He grinned teasingly. "I remember a time when you told me something different about my so-called intelligence."

"You're probably right," she agreed with a laugh.

The laughter seemed to ease the tension that had existed between them as they'd decorated the tree.

For the rest of the meal and through the cleanup afterward, they visited about mutual friends, spoke of movies they'd seen and talked about the kind of inconsequential things that held no emotional baggage for either one of them.

And throughout the rest of dinner, Seth found himself thinking back over their brief marriage, wondering how they had been so wrong about each other.

"Meghan, do you really think things might have been different between us if we'd talked more?" he asked as she placed the last plate into the dishwasher.

She hesitated a moment, staring down at the floor. "Yes…no…I don't know." She raised her gaze to meet his. "What difference does it make now? It's in the past and we can't go back, Seth. I don't want to go back." She lifted her chin, her eyes filled with defiance. "I've built a good life for myself and for Kirk."

"You never wonder what it would have been like if we'd stayed together?" he asked softly.

She shook her head, her red curls dancing with the vehemence of her movement. "I don't indulge in what-ifs. It's counterproductive. I didn't make you happy, and you didn't make me happy. We were smart to cut our losses and part."

He nodded, the unsettling edginess back inside him. Together they left the kitchen and went into the living room. The tree lit the room with magical color and the fire crackled cheerfully.

For just a moment Seth wished he could curl up on the sofa, Meghan in his arms and together they could watch their son play and laugh in delight as he watched the tree lights change colors.

He frowned. Meghan said her mother had once told her that Christmas brings on the crazies. Maybe it was true. His thoughts were definitely on the crazy side.

"Seth, I know I told you that you could sleep on the sofa while you're here, but if you want, you can take the spare bedroom."

"Are you sure? I don't want to overstep boundaries."

"I can handle you being in the spare room as well as I can handle you being on the sofa," she replied dryly.

"I thank you, but more importantly, my back thanks you." He picked up the black duffel bag he'd been living out of the past two days and started down the hallway.

"Seth?" Her voice stopped him and he turned back to her. "Some of your old clothes are hanging in the closet…if you need them…'' Her voice trailed off.

"Thanks, I packed pretty light, so they might come in handy." As he walked down the hall to the spare bedroom he wondered why she would keep anything that had belonged to him.

When he'd left, he'd left for good. Had it not been for Simon, he wouldn't have ever returned here. Or would he? One day would he have come back here to catch a glimpse of the wife he'd left behind? Just to check on her, make sure she was okay?

Eventually would he have come back to see Kirk? Would he have felt the need to connect with his son? To see what kind of man he'd become? He didn't know for sure, but liked to think he would have returned eventually.

When Seth reached the spare room it took him only minutes to unpack the few items from his bag. He opened the closet, surprised to discover old shirts, sweaters and pants hanging there. It would appear his ex-wife had gotten rid of nothing when he'd left.

By the time he returned to the living room, Meghan and Kirk had disappeared. Beneath the door of her office, he could see a light shining and knew she must have taken Kirk in there while she worked on the computer…worked to get him out of her house and out of her life.

He doused the fire to make sure it was safe for the night, then unplugged the tree lights. Finally, with nothing more to do, he went back into his bedroom and stretched out on the bed…thinking.

If he remained very still and listened, he could hear Kirk jabbering in the office. For some reason the sound filled him with a strange loneliness. It was an uncomfortable feeling, one he'd suffered often in the months right after he'd left Meghan.

The first month had been the worst. He'd been filled with an anger that bordered rage, felt as if life…love had betrayed him. And when she'd called at the end of that month and he'd heard her voice, he'd had a moment of rejoicing, certain she'd come to her senses and was calling to tell him to come home, he didn't have to quit his job.

Instead she had told him she was pregnant and never wanted him to see her again, wanted him to stay out of her life, out of their child's life.

The room was nearly dark, the only illumination was the unnatural light of the snow falling outside the window. He stared at the snow dancing past the window, his thoughts going back over the conversation with Meghan.

She'd been wrong when she'd said she hadn't made him happy. He'd been deliriously happy with Meghan. Until she'd asked the impossible from him.

He'd never dreamed that the moment he'd said "I do" to Meghan, she'd just assumed he'd soon be saying "I won't" to SPEAR. Maybe they should have talked more before getting married. Maybe if they had, he'd have realized he couldn't be the man she wanted…needed in her life.

He threw an arm across his eyes and instead focused on Simon, and all the things he'd do to the man before he turned him into SPEAR.

He'd make the bastard pay for all the agents who had died in the L.A. sting, make him pay for threatening the very fabric of the organization that had become family to Seth.

Seth closed his eyes and drew a deep breath, wondering how long he could remain in this house and not explode. He wanted Meghan. He wanted to make love to her, to taste her lips one more time, feel her naked body writhing beneath his.

But what he wanted wasn't fair, because he had no intention of changing anything. They were divorced, and they would remain so. He refused to quit his job for her, and she refused to stay with him as long as he was working as a field agent for SPEAR.

Stalemate.

He pulled off his clothes and tossed them to the floor, then crawled beneath the bedcovers. He closed his eyes, felt the fuzziness of sleep reaching out to claim him and gave into it, knowing sleep would certainly be more peaceful than his tumultuous thoughts.

Dreaming. He knew he was dreaming. It was his seventeenth birthday and he was walking home from school. It was a gorgeous late September day and the trees that lined the sidewalk had on their autumn colors. Reds, oranges and yellows…like the glow of birthday candles on a cake.

His mouth watered as he thought of the cake his mother had baked the night before. The house had filled with the scent of the chocolate cake and he'd watched her cover it with thick, gooey frosting.

As he walked, he wondered if his old man would remember that today was his birthday. Seth knew his father would be wrapped in an afghan, sitting in his chair and staring blankly at the television screen. In the past five years, the only time Seth saw his father get out of the chair was about nine o'clock each night when he would rise and shuffle off to bed.

Depression, that's what his mother had told him. His father was suffering from clinical depression. He'd seen doctors, talked to psychiatrists, tried an array of medications, but seemed to get worse rather than better.

Maybe today he'll actually look at me, ask me about my day, acknowledge that I exist in his world, Seth thought as he neared his house.

With each footstep that brought him closer to him, the unconscious Seth remained blithely unaware of the coming horror. But the part of Seth that knew he was dreaming, the part that still retained a small modicum of consciousness, knew...and fought against the inevitable.

Don't go inside, his subconscious screamed. Stay away from the house. And he watched in horror as the young Seth went around to the back door and entered the small house.

The cake was set on the counter and he thought about cutting himself a piece, but knew his mom would kill him if he didn't wait until after supper.

He placed his books on the table and that's when

he became aware of the smell. The scent of gunpowder…and death.

"Dad?" He walked into the living room and screamed.

"Seth! Seth, wake up."

He came instantly awake, the memory of blood and death lingering in his mind.

Meghan sat on the edge of the bed, visible in the light that spilled into the dark bedroom from the hallway. He jerked up, raked a hand through his hair and released a ragged breath.

"Are you all right?" Her voice was deep and low with concern.

"Yeah…I'm fine…just a nightmare. Sorry." He rubbed a hand across his eyes, attempting to shed the lingering horror of the dream. "What time is it?"

"A few minutes after eleven." She started to rise, but he grabbed her arm.

"Wait…" he said. "Please…stay for just a minute." He felt her hesitation, then she sat once again and he released her. "Did I wake you?"

"No. I was reading in bed."

He breathed deeply, savoring the feminine scent of lotion and perfume. It was a welcome change from the scents of his nightmare. "What about Kirk?"

"Still sleeping soundly." She hesitated, then continued, "Were you dreaming about the L.A. sting?"

"Yeah." It was easier to acknowledge that tragedy rather than deal with the ghosts of his distant past.

He couldn't imagine why he'd dreamed of his father's death. It had been years since he'd suffered the nightmares that had once plagued him nightly. He'd thought they were finally, truly behind him.

"You want to talk about it?"

A shiver worked through him, and he wasn't sure if it was the temperature of the room that made him cold, or the memory of his dream.

He wore only boxer shorts beneath the blankets, and knew by his brief touch of Meghan that she was clad in something long-sleeved and flannel. Probably pajamas. She'd always liked pajamas.

"You should be under the covers," she said, apparently noticing his shiver.

"You should turn up the furnace," he countered dryly.

She laughed, a low, sexy sound that instantly warmed him. "Seems like old times. The furnace fight was always predictable between us."

That wasn't the only predictable thing between them, Seth thought. Also predictable was their overwhelming passion for one another, a passion that suddenly stirred inside him.

In the darkness of the room, he could only see her silhouette, not her features. He leaned forward and reached out a hand and touched her hair. She went so still he thought she might not be breathing.

He said nothing, not knowing what to say, only knowing the need to touch her. His fingers left her hair and trailed across her jawline. His index finger raked across her lower lip and she opened her mouth slightly. He could feel her warm breath and it heightened the desire that raced through him.

Without questioning his action, without giving himself a chance to have second thoughts, he leaned forward and touched his lips to hers.

The contact was whisper soft, and he had no intention of deepening the kiss until he felt her lips part as if in anticipation.

He heard a groan, and was surprised to realize it came from him. Placing his hands on her shoulders, he pulled her closer, his mouth covering hers with a ravenous hunger.

He half expected her to protest, to pull away…slap his cheek…stomp out of the room in a temper. She did none of those things. Unexpectedly, she leaned into him, meeting his hunger with her own.

As she melted against him, he felt the thrust of her breasts beneath the thin flannel that separated them. He fought the impulse to reach up beneath her pajama top and capture their fullness and warmth in his palms.

Instead he tangled his hands in her hair, reveling in the silky strands that curled around his fingers. He loved the feel of her hair, the smell of it…a clean, slightly fruity scent.

He could drown in her, lose himself completely in the moist heat and sweetness of her mouth. His tongue darted against hers and he moved his hands from her hair to her shoulders.

Warm. His body temperature was rising at an alarming rate and he knew if he ran his hands inside her blouse, touched her bare skin, he'd be on fire and completely out of control.

Her hands moved across his bare chest, cool at first, but warming quickly as if filled with the heat from inside him.

Think. Even as their kiss continued and he felt her acquiescence in the depth of her response, in the fluid feel of her body against his, someplace in the back of his mind he knew he had to think about what he was doing.

If he made love to Meghan, things would only get more complicated. Nothing had changed between them. He still didn't understand the sacrifice she demanded he make, a sacrifice he refused to make.

"Meghan." He broke the kiss and raked his lips against the length of her throat. "My sweet Meghan. Let me make love to you."

"Yes." The single word hissed from her on a sweet sigh, and nearly drove him over the edge into the abyss of desire.

Once again his hands tangled in her hair as he rained tiny kisses across the hollow of her neck. "You never could cook worth a damn, and your housekeeping skills were spotty, but you were the best lover I ever had."

Rigid.

He didn't know how it was possible for a living, breathing human body to become so stiff. She was rigid for only a moment, then she flew into action. She slammed her hands into his chest, knocking him backward. He grunted as his head banged into the wall behind him.

"You are an insufferable bastard, Seth Greene," she exclaimed as she jumped off the bed.

He wished the lights were on, wished he could see the fire in those lovely eyes of hers, watch the freckles grow darker against the paling of her skin. She always paled when she was angry.

"As if I'd be interested in making love to you again," she scoffed disdainfully. "You were just fair as a lover, but since you left, I've certainly had better." She headed for the door. "And it will be a cold day in hell before you'll find me in your bed again."

Her exit would have been perfect…outraged, yet dignified, had she not stubbed her toe on the way out. She yelped and muttered a curse, then hobbled from the room. The hall light doused and a moment later he heard her bedroom door close.

He released a deep breath, willing his body to relax, fighting to forget the taste of Meghan that lingered in his mouth.

He'd done the right thing. He'd known his words would make her angry, would halt the quickening flood of desire that had threatened to drown them both.

Staring up at the ceiling, he waited for his ardor to cool. Making love to Meghan would be wonderful, gratifying and utterly wrong. He couldn't be the man she wanted, and she refused to accept the man he was.

So, why…knowing all this, did his body still yearn for hers? Christmas crazies. It was the only rational answer.

# Chapter 7

Meghan wasn't sure which hurt worse, her toe or her pride. She suspected she might have broken her little toe. The nail was half torn away and it had swelled up to twice its normal size. But that injury was relatively insignificant next to her bruised and bloody pride.

And she wasn't sure who she was more angry with, Seth or herself.

As she got into her own bed, her body still burned and her stomach ached with the need for fulfillment. It had been so long…so achingly long since she'd felt the warmth of male arms surrounding her, the heat of hungry lips against hers.

And the thing that made her most angry was that she didn't want just any arms around her. She didn't want just any lips on hers.

Seth. She wanted him—his arms, his mouth, *him* taking possession of her body and soul. She frowned. No, not her soul. Never again her soul. She'd given that to him once before, and he'd disregarded her gift and left her completely bereft.

So, why did she still want him?

She certainly refused to contemplate that she might still harbor any love for him.

Familiarity. Surely that was the answer. Seth was the devil she knew, and she knew how utterly wonderful sex was with him.

Inwardly fuming, his words echoed in her head. Couldn't cook, wasn't much of a housekeeper… surely he knew her well enough to know such sentiments spoken by him would make her mad.

Turning over on her back, she stared at the darkened ceiling. So, why had he said such things? He'd spoken those words intentionally to anger her. There was no other reasonable explanation.

He'd said them because he hadn't really wanted to make love to her.

The realization struck her like a slap upside the head. He didn't want her. He didn't want her cooking his meals, cleaning his house, but most importantly, he didn't want her in his bed.

A door she hadn't realized was partially opened, slammed shut in her heart. The resounding bang of that door closing caused pain to shoot through her. The knowledge that he didn't want to make love to her ever again ached deep within her.

By the time she awakened the next morning, the

ache was almost gone, buried beneath a healthy dose of anger. The sun was shining through her bedroom window with the promise of a beautiful, clear winter day. And with the sunshine came a clearing of her thoughts.

As Meghan dressed she thought of those moments in Seth's bed, when desire had flared nearly out of control.

It had been a momentary lapse in judgment, brought on by the intimacy of the snow falling and the cracking fire, the emotional pleasure of decorating the tree with Seth and Kirk. The family facade had temporarily unsettled her, made her vulnerable.

But the sun was melting the snow, just as the incident last night had dissolved any lingering belief that there could ever be anything between herself and Seth.

He didn't want her and she certainly didn't want to be with a man who didn't want her. But she couldn't help still feeling angry when she thought of the insensitive words he'd uttered to chase her from his bed.

She carried her anger as a shield as she left her room. She checked on Kirk, surprised to find him still sleeping, then went into the kitchen.

Seth sat at the table, a cup of coffee before him. He was dressed in his usual pair of jeans and a gray sweater she recognized from the spare room closet.

"Good morning," he said as she entered the kitchen. She didn't reply. "How's your toe?" he asked. A tiny smile played at the corner of his lips, as if he'd found her clumsy, painful exit from his room the night before immensely amusing.

She was not amused. "It's fine." She poured herself a cup of coffee and contemplated going into her office to work. Instead, feeling as if to retreat would somehow be a victory for him, she joined him at the table.

She sipped her coffee and shot him a surreptitious glance over the rim of her mug. He looked well rested, as if he'd slept the sleep of the innocent. And she knew she looked haggard, having tossed and turned for most of the night.

"Kirk still asleep?" he asked.

"Yes, I checked on him a few minutes ago." She frowned. "It's unusual for him to sleep in. I hope he isn't getting sick."

"We probably just wore him out yesterday with the tree decorating."

"Probably," she agreed, then took another sip of her coffee.

She wanted to ask him about his nightmares. In the seven months they had been married, she couldn't remember Seth ever suffering a nightmare.

Granted, the L.A. sting operation had been a failure, and some of their agents had been killed and wounded, but Seth had been involved in operations before that had been dismal failures and resulted in deaths.

Besides, if his nightmare had really been about the L.A. sting, then why had the tortured cry that had pulled her from her bed to his sounded like a mournful wail of the word "dad"?

She was trying to figure out how to ask him about it when Kirk awakened. She left the table and hurried into the bedroom where Kirk stood in his crib, crying plaintively for attention.

"Mama," he said, tears magically stopping as he lifted his arms toward her.

"Okay, big guy." She grabbed a clean diaper from the bag on the dresser, then changed Kirk and put him in a red turtleneck and a pair of denim overalls.

"You want some breakfast?" she asked as she carried him down the hall to the kitchen. "How about an egg and some toast."

"Toast," he echoed and nodded his head. Meghan's heart clenched as she realized his sober little expression made him look amazingly like Seth.

When she'd been carrying Kirk, she'd steadfastly refused to dwell on thoughts of the man who had sired him. She'd pretended Kirk had been the result of a miracle, or an anonymous donor from a sperm bank. He was hers...and nobody else had anything to do with him.

But seeing Seth and Kirk together, there was no way to deny Seth's genes, no way to pretend Kirk had come from any other source than from Seth.

When they returned to the kitchen, Meghan scrambled an egg and made toast for Kirk while Seth entertained the little boy by making silly faces.

The kitchen filled with the sounds of Kirk's merriment as he and Seth played a game of peekaboo.

Meghan placed Kirk's plate before him, effectively ending the games.

"I don't get any breakfast?" Seth asked when she once again sat at the table.

She raised an eyebrow. "Now why would you want a woman who can't cook to make you anything to eat?" She was satisfied by the slight red that swept over his face.

He sipped his coffee, then set the cup on the table. "I noticed one of the shelves in the bookcase in the living room is missing."

She nodded, surprised by his abrupt change of topic. "It needs some nails driven in. I just haven't taken the time to do it."

"I'd be glad to fix it for you."

She knew what he was doing. Trying to apologize for his words the night before. She shrugged, as if not caring one way or the other. "If you want to fix it, the shelf is in the hall closet."

He sighed and stared into his coffee cup. "Meghan...about last night..."

"There's nothing to talk about," she interrupted him. "Everything you said was true. I'm not a great cook and I don't really care about hunting down every dust bunny in the house." She eyed him boldly, defiantly. "But I am terrific in bed."

He grinned, his eyes twinkling wickedly. "At least on that we both agree."

"Oh heavens, I've improved greatly since our divorce," she exclaimed, satisfied when his eyes widened slightly. The doorbell chiming was a welcome interruption.

Meghan hurried to answer it. She wanted Seth to believe that life and love had gone on for her after he'd left, but if he dug too deeply, he'd realize there had never been another man who had been able to touch her as deeply, as profoundly as he had.

She opened the front door. ''David,'' she said in surprise.

''Hi, Meghan. I was doing a little last minute shopping and decided to drop in and see if you'd offer a weary shopper a cup of coffee.'' He smiled, his brown eyes warm, but uncertain.

Meghan hesitated, unsure what to do about Seth. At that moment the object of her concern stepped up next to her at the door. David's smile faded, the uncertainty in his eyes growing deeper.

''Hello.'' Seth stuck out his hand and in his expression Meghan saw a hint of challenge. ''I'm Meghan's...''

''Cousin,'' Meghan exclaimed. ''My cousin, Steve.''

She'd had a feeling Seth had been going to introduce himself as her ex-husband. She wasn't sure if she'd introduced him as Steve to protect him or simply to irritate him.

The uncertainty in David's eyes faded and he gripped Seth's hand and gave him a friendly smile. ''Well, it's nice to meet a member of Meghan's family.''

"Come on in, I've got the coffee on," Meghan said.

"Pretty early to be out shopping," Seth observed as they walked through the living room.

"Not many shopping days left until Christmas. Besides, the early bird gets the best pick of sale items," David replied.

"Da!" Kirk grinned broadly at David as they entered the kitchen.

"Hey, little guy." David chucked Kirk beneath his chin and Meghan saw Seth's features grow taut. Meghan watched Seth deftly maneuver himself between David and Kirk.

He's jealous. The realization stunned Meghan. Seth was jealous.

As she poured David a cup of coffee, he sat down in one of the chairs at the table. "So, are you visiting Meghan for the holidays?" he asked Seth.

"Steve comes to visit whenever he's between jobs," Meghan said. She smiled sweetly at Seth, whose features were growing more tense. "He visits fairly often. Of course, I don't mind, him being family and all."

"That's nice. It's good for family to take care of family," David said with a friendly smile. "I miss having family around during the holidays. All of mine are out in California."

"Plane tickets are fairly cheap," Seth said evenly. "You could always go there."

"True," David agreed. "But I also really enjoy being home during the holidays."

"Sounds like a Christmas song," Meghan said as she placed a cup of coffee in front of the pleasant-looking, sandy-haired man.

"So, what sort of business are you in, David?" Seth leaned against the center island and eyed the man at the table.

"Accounting," David replied. "I head my own accounting firm here in D.C."

"Sounds fascinating," Seth said, and Meghan wondered if David picked up on Seth's sarcasm.

David laughed good-naturedly. "Of course it isn't fascinating. In fact, most of the time it's dreadfully boring. But I make a lot of money working nine to five and never have to bring my work home with me."

"Speaking of work." Meghan turned to Seth and sent him a pointed glare. "Weren't you going to see about fixing that shelf in the living room for me?"

Seth frowned. "You mean right now?"

Meghan smiled sweetly and nodded. "I really appreciate it, Steve."

She wasn't sure why, but it was obvious Seth didn't want to leave the kitchen. She knew it couldn't be that he was somehow jealous about David and her. He'd made it clear the night before he didn't want her.

Kirk. That was the only explanation. Seth was afraid that somehow David might find a place in his son's life when he had no place in Kirk's life.

She steeled her heart against an ache that suddenly appeared. Seth had made his choice, and she had made hers. Eventually Meghan wanted to marry again. She wanted to build a family for Kirk, for herself. And if and when that happened, Seth would just have to deal with it.

With a nod to David, Seth left the kitchen, and Meghan wondered how it was possible for the man who had broken her heart to still somehow retain possession of the remaining pieces?

Seth didn't like him. As he found the shelf in the hall closet, he thought of the man seated at the kitchen table.

He conceded that David wasn't a bad-looking man, if one liked the pale, intellectual type. Still, he hadn't liked the way David's eyes had played on Meghan. Seth recognized the look...sheer hunger.

With a frown, Seth went into the utility room and located a tape measure, an old hammer and a coffee can filled with nails.

Meghan had certainly been quick to introduce him as cousin Steve. She'd obviously not wanted David to know she was sharing her home with her ex-husband.

Aggravation ripped through him. She'd made him sound like some unemployed bum sponging off her. Not that he cared what dear David thought of him.

David, who'd sent her a gorgeous arrangement of flowers. She'd taken a cooking class with the man, prepared a home-cooked meal for him.

Had she also slept with him? Had she perfected her skill as a lover with the man now sitting at the kitchen table? The thought twisted in Seth's gut in spite of the fact he knew he had no right to speculate on her love life.

David had a job that Meghan would consider suitable for husband material...a job that would have him home for supper every night, where the only danger he faced was a paper cut.

Seth returned to the living room, his frown deepening as he heard Meghan's musical laughter wafting from the kitchen. When was the last time he'd made her laugh like that?

It didn't take Seth long to fix the shelf. When he was finished, his first desire was to return to the kitchen, break up the little family scene that seemed to be going on.

Instead, he sat down on the sofa, trying to ignore the sounds of Meghan's laughter, David's low rumble and Kirk's uninhibited chatter.

He hadn't come back here to interfere in her personal life. He'd run back here because he'd needed her professional help, nothing more, nothing less.

So, why did he hate the idea of David sitting in his kitchen, laughing with his son...perhaps kissing his wife? Stroking those evocative freckles?

He could only hope that David's kiss was as boring as his job. As this thought crossed his mind, Seth instantly felt mean-spirited and small. Why should he begrudge Meghan a chance at happiness? Why should he resent a man who could make her happy where he had failed?

He had no answer.

It was nearly two hours later that David finally left. "Did you have a nice visit?" Seth asked as she closed the door behind the tall accountant. He shut off the television he'd been watching and got up from the sofa.

"He's a very nice man," she said. She placed Kirk on the living room floor, then straightened.

"I noticed his hairline was getting pretty thin. He'll probably be bald within the next five years." Seth had the feeling his mouth had been possessed by a spoiled adolescent male.

Meghan smiled. "I've always found bald men rather sexy."

"Since when?" he challenged her statement.

"Since you mentioned it." Her gaze swept toward the bookcase. "Thanks for fixing the shelf."

"You're welcome." He studied her features, noting the flush of color that dotted her cheeks. Had David's presence created that attractive blush?

He shoved his hands in his pockets, afraid if he didn't do something with them, they would be all over her. "Don't forget, we're supposed to go next door this evening," he said.

What he wanted to say was that he was sorry for his words the night before, that he wished they could replay last night and the outcome would be far different.

He wished he could take her in his arms, capture her lips with his, stroke fire into her veins. He wanted to caress her until she made those throaty little moans that drove him wild. He wanted to ease into her warmth and feel her hands clutch his back as he carried them both to the brink of shattering.

He stared at her, knew his hunger was in his eyes for her to see. And she stared back at him, her eyes widening as she unconsciously wet her lips with the tip of her tongue.

Seth took a step toward her, wanting to cover those lips with his own, needing her to need him. He recognized at that moment that although he'd left Meghan, although they'd agreed to part and had divorced, he'd never really gotten her out of his system.

She was an itch he had to scratch, a sore that hadn't healed, a piece of his past that refused to release him.

He stepped closer, close enough to see the brilliant green and gold flecks of her eyes. He was close enough now that if he reached out, he could touch her…caress her soft skin.

He had the feeling that if he could just hold her in his arms one last time, make love to her once more, then he'd be able to get her out of his head. The last time they'd made love, neither of them had been aware that it was an experience they'd never share again.

She took a step toward him, and in his peripheral vision, Seth saw the Christmas tree tilt precariously to the right.

For just a brief moment, he wondered if perhaps his need to hold Meghan had made him dizzy. Then he realized what was happening.

"Kirk!" he exclaimed, louder than he'd intended. The moment between Seth and Meghan was broken as Seth darted forward to stop the little boy before he upended the whole tree.

Kirk froze, his chubby hand filled with tree limb. As Seth grabbed his hand from the tree and snatched him up into his arms, Kirk let out a yowl.

"You frightened him," Meghan exclaimed as she took the crying child from his arms. She patted Kirk's back and glared at Seth.

"He frightened me," Seth replied defensively. "I was afraid he was going to bring the tree down on top of his head."

Kirk cried louder, as if aware of the tension that suddenly rippled the air between the two adults.

"You didn't have to be so harsh." Her eyes sparkled with anger, and Seth wondered if she were really that angry for him yelling at Kirk, or angry because for just a moment she'd wanted him with the same intensity that he'd wanted her.

"I didn't mean to be harsh," Seth said softly.

Meghan kissed Kirk's forehead, then nodded at Seth. "Okay. Sorry I overreacted. He needs a diaper change and maybe a nap." She turned and left the room.

Within minutes Kirk's crying had stopped and Seth heard Meghan leave the nursery and go into her office. He knew what she was doing...working...seeking Simon...attempting to find the information that would remove Seth from her life. The problem was...Seth wasn't so sure he wanted to be removed.

# Chapter 8

"This is so nice." Rose Columbus beamed at Meghan and Seth as they seated themselves at her kitchen table. She'd greeted them at the door, clad in a red and green duster, a brilliant smile wreathing her face. As she'd led them through the cluttered living room, they'd been enveloped by the warm, sweet scents of cinnamon and spices.

"Now, what can I get you both to drink? I have eggnog and punch. The punch has a little extra kick to it."

"Eggnog sounds lovely," Meghan said, her attention torn between the plump older woman and Kirk, who careened around the kitchen obviously looking for something to get into.

"I'll try some of that holiday punch with the kick," Seth said with a devilish wink at Rose.

She giggled girlishly. "Somehow I knew that's what you'd choose." She poured the drinks and set them on the table. "I'm so pleased you all decided to accept my invitation. I don't get much company anymore." Her plump cheeks were flushed with pleasure as she joined them at the table.

"No, no, Kirk," Meghan exclaimed as Kirk opened one of the cabinet doors.

"He's all right," Rose assured her. "That's my pots and pans cabinet. I've never known a little tot who didn't love to play with pots and pans."

Meghan nodded and tried to relax, but relaxation was impossible…had been impossible since that moment earlier in the day with Seth in the living room.

As Seth and Rose talked about Christmas and the weather, Meghan thought of that moment, when Seth's eyes had been filled with a hunger that had left her breathless…almost senseless.

If he didn't really want her, then why did he look at her as if she were the last morsel of food left on the planet and he was a starving survivor?

He confused her, and she didn't like it one single bit. She also didn't like the way her senses were intensely heightened and she felt as if she might jump out of her own skin at any minute.

He had to go. The three days she'd promised him were up and she couldn't stand feeling the way she did. It was time for him to go.

"Please, help yourself to the goodies," Rose said, gesturing to a platter of cookies in the center of the table.

Meghan reached for one at the same time Seth did. Their hands met, fingers touching. Meghan jerked hers back as electrical currents raced through her hand, traveled the length of her arm and lodged in a ball of heat in the pit of her stomach.

"Sorry," she muttered and felt the heat of a blush sweep across her cheeks. She waited until he had a cookie, then took one for herself.

"You mentioned the other day that the two of you are cousins…on which side?" Rose asked curiously.

"Mother's," Meghan said.

"Father's," Seth replied at the same time.

"Indeed." Rose's gray eyebrows danced up on her broad forehead.

"It's actually rather complicated," Seth said with a forced laugh. "We aren't first cousins and we have a rather tangled family tree."

"It sounds more than tangled," Rose exclaimed with a short bark of laughter. "It sounds like a regular jungle." She eyed them in speculation, and Meghan had a feeling she didn't believe them at all.

Kirk carried a small saucepan toward Seth. "Da…" he said and handed it to Seth.

Seth leaned down and took the pan, his eyes lit with intense love. "Pan," Seth said to the little boy.

Kirk grinned. "Pa…" He took it back from Seth, then returned to his seat on the floor in front of the cabinet and pulled out another pan.

"He's taken to you," Rose observed.

Seth smiled, looking as handsome as Meghan had

ever seen him. "I've definitely taken to him," he replied. "He's a pretty special little guy."

"That's good." Rose nodded her head, her gray curls dancing with the motion. "A boy needs a man's influence in his life. Of course, a father's influence would be best, but I guess that's out of the question where Kirk is concerned. According to Meghan, Kirk's daddy was nothing more than an irresponsible sperm donor."

Again Meghan felt her cheeks flush hotly and she kept her gaze carefully averted from Seth. She'd said lots of things to Rose about her ex-husband when Rose had first moved in. It had only been a few months since the divorce and Meghan was still reeling from bitterness and pain.

"I'd say Meghan's characterization of her exhusband might be a bit biased," Seth replied dryly.

"Oh, you know him?" Rose leaned forward eagerly.

"He's one of my closest friends."

Rose inched closer to Seth, her eyes lit with the thrill of discovery. "Is he really as handsome as Meghan described him to me?"

"Rose," Meghan squeaked in faint protest.

"Dear Meghan, I'm an old woman. I live vicariously." Rose directed her attention back to Seth. "Well? Is he?"

Seth grinned, obviously enjoying the topic of conversation while Meghan fought her need to scream in utter frustration.

"Why don't you tell me exactly what Meghan has

told you about her ex husband, and I'll tell you if it's really true," Seth replied with a lazy grin.

"Bedroom eyes." Rose looked at Meghan for confirmation. "You remember you told me he has eyes that make a woman forget everything except falling into bed with him. She said looking into his eyes could make a woman forget her own name, or what day of the week it was."

Seth looked at Meghan. "You said that?"

"Is this really necessary?" Meghan protested, refusing to answer his question.

She wasn't sure who she wanted to strangle... Rose for having a big mouth, or herself for having an even bigger one in spilling such things to Rose at one time.

"Probably not, but it's lots of fun," Seth replied, his eyes green seas of mischief. "I'll tell you what, we'll gossip about your ex, then we can gossip about mine."

"You're divorced, too, Steve?" Rose leaned back in her chair and sighed mournfully. "You young folks marry at the drop of a hat and divorce just as quickly. Doesn't anyone work at staying married anymore?"

Her question hung in the air. It wasn't answered, not by Seth, who downed the last of his punch, nor by Meghan, who focused her attention on the cookie in her hand.

Seth set his glass back on the table and raked a hand through his hair, his cocky smile gone. "Sometimes, in a marriage, there's just nothing to work with. Sometimes the expectations of one person in the relationship are too high, too unrealistic. Sometimes one of the people in the relationship just wants too much.''

His gaze locked with Meghan's. She was surprised to see a flicker of hurt and the dark vestiges of anger in the depths of his eyes. She averted her gaze from his.

''And sometimes a marriage is built on lust and when the lust fades, there's nothing left to build on.'' Meghan truly believed in her heart that's what had happened to her marriage where Seth was concerned.

He'd wanted her...he'd lusted for her, but when the lust had waned, he hadn't been willing to make the kind of commitment, the kind of concession that would assure them a real marriage.

At that moment, Kirk began to fuss. He crawled toward Meghan, who scooped him up in her arms and offered him a cookie. She was aware of Rose watching both her and Seth speculatively.

''So, have you two gotten your Christmas shopping finished?'' Rose asked.

''I didn't do much shopping,'' Meghan said, grateful for the change in topic. ''Kirk is still small enough that he's more interested in the wrapping paper than what lies beneath it. I picked him up a couple of educational toys that I thought he might enjoy.''

''What about you, Steve? Have you finished your shopping?''

''Not yet,'' Seth replied. ''Kirk will be easy to buy

for, but Meghan may prove a problem.'' He grinned
easily. ''What do you buy for a self-sufficient woman
who has everything she wants?''

*I don't have everything I want. I don't have you.*
The words in her brain horrified her. She didn't want
to want Seth, not ever again. ''You don't have to
buy me anything,'' she protested. ''After all, you
won't even be here for Christmas. You said you'd
only be here for three days. Today is your last day,
isn't it?'' Seth's eyes narrowed at her words.

''Surely you can see your way to stay until after
Christmas,'' Rose protested.

Seth shrugged and grabbed another cookie from
the plate. ''It's really up to Meghan. I'm here strictly
because of her hospitality.''

Rose smiled. ''And of course she wouldn't want
you to spend the holidays all alone.'' Rose turned
her attention to Meghan, who was wrestling a fussy
Kirk in her lap. ''Meghan is the sweetest woman I
know. I'm sure she wouldn't mind if you extended
your stay.''

Meghan wasn't sweet, and she was growing less
sweet by the moment. She'd made up her mind. Tonight was Seth's last night in her house. She couldn't
handle his presence any longer. He made her weak,
made her think of things she shouldn't dwell on,
stirred emotions she refused to entertain.

As Seth and Rose continued a conversation about
favorite Christmas movies, Meghan struggled with
Kirk, who continued to fuss, not wanting the cookie
she'd given him and wiggling with discontent on her

lap. He'd been rather cranky all day. Probably cutting more teeth, she thought.

Kirk finally settled against her and calmed down. Meghan stroked his hair and found her gaze once again on Seth.

He was wearing another of the sweaters from the spare room closet, this one a deep forest green that intensified the color of his eyes.

Bedroom eyes. Intense green, with thick, long dark lashes, Seth's eyes definitely made Meghan think of twisted sheets, languid caresses and hot sex.

She'd bought him that sweater when she'd been in the first throes of a love so intense it had ached inside her. And that was an emotion she never wanted to feel again…an emotion that threatened to return the longer he remained in her world.

He had to leave tomorrow, despite the fact that she hadn't been able to give him the information he needed to find Simon. She just couldn't risk loving him again.

Kirk stirred, whining pitifully and leaning his head against her chest.

"I've never seen that baby so fussy," Rose said.

"It is unusual," Meghan agreed. "He must be teething." Meghan stood, with Kirk in her arms. "If you will excuse me for a moment, maybe he needs a diaper change." She grabbed the diaper bag they'd brought with them and left the kitchen.

She laid Kirk down on the living room floor and set to changing his diaper. When she took off his wet one, she frowned as she saw a red rash on his stomach. She put a fresh diaper on him, then pulled up his shirt, noticing that the rash also covered his chest and under his arms. She also realized he felt unusually warm.

She redressed him, then carried him back into the kitchen. "He has a rash," she said worriedly. "And I think he's running a fever."

Rose stood, as did Seth. "Let me see that baby," Rose exclaimed. Rose took the fussy boy from Meghan's arms and sat back down with him on her lap. She pulled up his shirt, then checked his face and neck. "It's nothing to be too concerned about, this little munchkin has chicken pox."

Meghan stared at Rose in horror, unsure whether to laugh or to cry.

"Meghan, this is not the time to throw me out," Seth exclaimed. They had just returned from Rose's place and Meghan was pacing the living room with a fussing Kirk in her arms.

"Seth, I gave you three days and the three days are up." Meghan stopped her pacing and sat on the sofa, trying to soothe Kirk.

Seth sat down next to her. "Meghan, please think about what you're doing."

"I have thought about it," she countered. "You can take a motel room. I'll continue to try to find the information you need."

"And how are you going to do that?" he asked gently.

She shifted Kirk's position on her lap and looked

at Seth curiously. "What do you mean, how am I going to do that? I'll keep looking."

"So, you're going to take Kirk into day care tomorrow?"

He could tell she hadn't thought that far ahead by the look of horror that crossed her face. "I...I can't do that," she said, worry etching a crease in her forehead. "They won't take him with chicken pox."

"Exactly my point. Meghan, you need me now."

Her brow wrinkled with impatience. "Seth, you may be able to do a lot of things, but you can't make chicken pox miraculously disappear," she scoffed.

"No, but what I can do is keep Kirk here with me while you go to work."

"No, that's just not a good idea."

Seth saw her arms tighten around Kirk, who'd finally fallen into an exhausted sleep. Anger swept through him. "Why isn't it a good idea?" he asked curtly. "Do you think I'm not capable of caring for him? Are you afraid somehow I'll hurt him?"

"Of course not," she replied and looked away from him. The frown across her forehead deepened and she stood. "He's sleeping now. I'm going to put him in bed."

Seth watched her go, knew she was attempting to escape the conversation, but he didn't intend to allow her to escape. He'd come here seeking her help, and for the last three days he'd felt useless, without purpose.

But now he felt as if he'd been handed a mission...to care take for his son, the son he knew now he would never be able to walk away from. He and Meghan would never again be a couple, but Seth would always be a father.

However, he knew this particular argument would have to wait for another day, another time. He'd fight this first battle before he took on the entire war.

He stood and paced the room, waiting for her to return to the living room. When she finally came back, she held her shoulders defensively straight and he knew she intended to go to battle.

She walked over to the bookcase and straightened a row of paperbacks, obviously gathering her thoughts or waiting for him to speak first.

He didn't. He watched her and waited.

She finally turned to face him, a weary expression on her face. "Seth, I don't want to fight."

"Then don't fight me on this," he countered. He stepped toward her, reached out and took her hands in his. "Let me do this, Meghan." She tried to pull her hands from his, but he held tight. "Let me do it for you...for myself."

"Seth, please..." She pulled her hands again, and this time he released them.

Seth sighed in frustration. "There are only seven more days until the Christmas holiday. Seven days, Meghan. Let me take care of him. We're not talking about forever here...just seven days." They'd talk about forever later, he promised himself. "Hopefully by then, you'll have the information I need and I'll be out of here."

She chewed her bottom lip and threaded several

fingers through her hair. "All right," she finally relented. "We'll try it for tomorrow. But you might find a sick little boy is far more difficult to handle than any assignment SPEAR could ever give you."

"I'm sure we'll be fine," Seth said, a thrill surging through him as he thought of spending quality time with his son.

At that moment, as if to protest Seth's words of confidence, Kirk cried.

He fussed off and on all night long. Seth heard Meghan up and down several times before he went into the nursery to offer to take over.

"No, I'm fine," Meghan said. She sat in the rocking chair in Kirk's room, rocking back and forth with Kirk in her arms. "You'd better save your strength for tomorrow."

Seth had left the room, but had lingered in the hallway, listening to the squeak of the rocking chair and Meghan's sweet voice humming a lullaby to Kirk.

Reluctantly, Seth had gone back to his room.

At dawn he got out of bed and put the coffee on, eager for his day with Kirk to begin. By six-thirty, Meghan entered the kitchen with Kirk in her arms.

Although she was already dressed and ready for work, she looked exhausted. "I changed his diaper, but left him in his pajamas," she said as she put him in his high chair. His face was spotty, but he offered Seth a smile.

"It's still early," Seth said. "Sit down and have a cup of coffee."

She shook her head. "I need to get in early... before Mark gets there. I'll grab coffee at work." She grabbed a slip of paper from one of the drawers, then dug a pen from her purse. "Here's my number at work." She scribbled a number, then handed him the slip of paper. "Call me if there are any problems." She frowned thoughtfully. "Make sure you keep him changed, and if he gets too fussy, you might try a lukewarm bath." She pointed to a small bottle on the counter. "There's a fever-reducing medicine you can give him every four hours."

"I'm sure we'll be fine," he assured her. He got up from the table and walked with her to the front door. "Don't worry," he said.

She turned at the door, a sardonic smile twisting her lips. "Worry is what mothers do best."

He placed his hands on her shoulders and fought the impulse to pull her against his chest, let her lean against him. "For today, this mother doesn't have to worry. We'll be fine here."

She nodded and without a backward glance, flew out the door. At that moment Kirk wailed from the kitchen.

"Don't worry."

Seth's words rang in Meghan's ears as she drove to her office. How could she help but worry? Her son was sick with chicken pox and she'd left him in the care of a man she hadn't wanted in his life.

She should have kicked Seth off her front porch

the moment he'd arrived. She should have never agreed to help him, never allowed him even a toehold in their lives. She had a feeling after today, he'd not only have a toe in the door, he'd have his entire foot.

With every minute of every day that had passed, she'd seen the bonding going on with Kirk and Seth, saw the immense love that sparked in Seth's eyes each time his gaze landed on his son. He was not going to walk away as he'd promised.

No matter how quickly she found him the information about Simon, it wouldn't be quick enough to stop the inevitable change that would now occur in her life. And Meghan dreaded this particular change.

If Seth refused to leave Kirk's life, then he would forever be in hers. Not as a husband, not as a lover, but as Kirk's father. She would have to see him, talk to him, share custody of Kirk with him, and not let her heart be touched.

As she got out of her car, the residual snow beneath her feet crackled with ice that had reformed during the night. There would be no further melting today. The wind whistled straight from the north and bit at exposed skin.

Once inside the office, she shrugged out of her coat, quickly made a pot of coffee, then booted up her computer. She checked her wristwatch, then poured herself a cup of the fresh brew and sat down at her desk. It was just after seven. If she were lucky, she'd get an hour or so in working to find signs of Simon and his drug cache before Mark came into work for the day.

Taking a sip of her coffee, she began the search.

"Are you bucking for a bonus?"

Meghan squeaked in surprise and guiltily hit the button that instantly blanked her screen. "Mark! I didn't hear you come in."

"Obviously." He took off his coat, his gaze narrowed on her in speculation. "You're in terribly early again." He hung his coat on the wooden coat tree, his gaze not leaving her. "If I remember right, you came in real early last Friday, too."

"Did I?" Meghan forced a light laugh and got up to get another cup of coffee. "I've just been getting up and around earlier I guess."

The sudden, shrill ring of the phone startled her. She dropped the cup. The ceramic shattered, spewing coffee all over the floor.

As Mark grabbed the phone, she quickly cleaned up her mess. She relaxed somewhat as she realized the caller apparently wasn't Seth. When she straightened, she found Mark's gaze on her once again.

"Is everything all right, Meghan?" he asked, a faint shadow of suspicion in his eyes.

"Of course it is," she instantly replied, fighting back a growing wall of guilt and a sudden desire to cry.

Of course everything is fine. I'm harboring a SPEAR fugitive in my house, searching files I don't belong in to help him. He's watching my son who has chicken pox and if I'm not careful, I think I could fall in love with him all over again.

''Is there anything you need to talk about?'' Mark pressed.

Meghan's heart thundered in her chest. Did Mark suspect she was hiding something? Had he somehow guessed that Seth was at her house? ''Is something on your mind, Mark?'' she countered, forcing herself to look him square in the eye.

He held her gaze for a long moment, then shrugged. ''Nope, guess not. You just seem a little edgy this morning. And I noticed you seemed sort of uptight the other day, as well.''

Meghan poured herself a fresh cup of coffee, then turned back to look at Mark. ''It's Kirk. He has the chicken pox.''

The stress that had lined Mark's forehead instantly dissipated. ''Why didn't you say something?'' he said, obviously relieved by her reply. He poured himself a cup of coffee and sprawled in the chair at his desk. ''So, how is the little tyke?''

''Spotty and cranky.'' Relief flooded through Meghan. ''I came in early this morning thinking maybe I can scoot out of here early this afternoon.''

''Sure, I don't see why not.'' Again there was a whisper of suspicion in Mark's eyes. ''Of course, it's going to be kind of hard to get your work done if you keep your computer screen blanked out all the time.''

A nervous giggle escaped Meghan. ''Oh...I was just...playing solitaire.'' The lie sounded lame, but it was the only thing she could come up with. She'd never been very good at subterfuge.

Mark took a sip of his coffee and she felt his gaze studying her as she pulled up her work for the day. "Meghan, you aren't having any financial problems, are you?"

She looked at him in surprise. "No...why?"

"Just curious." He took a sip of his coffee. "If you were having problems...any sort of problems, you know you can talk to me, right?"

"Sure," she agreed hesitantly. He nodded, as if satisfied he'd said what was needed and Meghan focused her attention on her computer screen.

It wasn't until a few minutes later she realized what Mark was worried about. The questions about her finances, the suspicion in his eyes.

Terrific, she thought irritably. Her co-worker suspected she was either spying for another government agency...or selling out to foreign interests. In any case, he suspected her of being a traitor. Could life possibly get any more complicated?

## Chapter 9

As soon as Meghan left, Seth turned up the heat in the house, grateful when warm air suffused the rooms. The woman had no blood, he thought as he raced back into the kitchen, where Kirk awaited him.

Seth scrambled eggs for Kirk as Meghan had done the morning before. Only unlike the morning before, this morning Kirk refused to eat.

He mashed the eggs between his fingers, then rubbed them in his hair. He slid them across the tray and dropped little pieces of them from his plate to the floor.

Seth watched helplessly, unsure whether to remove the eggs from his high chair tray or leave them and hope that some of the breakfast would accidentally manage to get into Kirk's mouth. It wasn't until

Kirk began throwing the eggs at Seth that Seth called an end to breakfast.

"Okay buddy, that's it," he said as he lifted Kirk out of the high chair. Kirk laid his head against Seth's chest and despite the eggs' mess that smashed against Seth's shirt, an explosion of love burst in his heart.

He ached for all the time he'd already missed with Kirk. The first moment of birth, of his first smile…the first word…the first step. So many momentous firsts already missed and never to be recaptured.

But still plenty more to come and as Kirk smiled up at Seth, Seth realized there was no way in hell he could walk away from this child…his child.

He carried Kirk into the bathroom where he did his best to scrub away all traces of the breakfast not eaten. Kirk fought his efforts. "No," he said and shoved at the washcloth. "No, no." Kirk pushed against Seth, displaying a show of surprising strength.

Seth ignored his protests and finished the task, although pride soared inside him. He liked that his son already had a mind of his own and didn't seem reluctant to express it.

However, his pride lasted only a little while, concern replacing it. As the morning wore on, Kirk fussed almost continuously. He was warm with fever and obviously uncomfortable. But it was too soon to give him more fever-reducing medicine.

Seth dragged half the toys from the bedroom into

the living room floor in an effort to entertain him. Seth built with the blocks, contorted his face into funny expressions, he did everything but stand on his head in an attempt to make Kirk happy. And when all else failed, he did stand on his head, the actions producing the first giggle of the day from the sick little boy.

However, the giggle lasted only a moment, then Kirk began to fuss again…a monotonous wail without tears that ripped at Seth's heart.

He considered calling Meghan to see if she had any advice on what he should do to ease Kirk's obvious discomfort, but instantly dismissed the idea. The last thing he wanted her to think was that he couldn't take care of his own son….sick or not.

Still, he'd faced the devil a thousand times in his work, had suffered a gunshot wound that had nearly killed him, but nothing had prepared him for how to make a sick little boy feel better.

The doorbell rang near lunchtime. Seth went to the door and peered out the peephole, relieved to see Rose Columbus standing on the porch.

"Rose," he greeted her eagerly, wondering if she heard the desperation in his voice. "Please, come in."

"Tough morning?" she asked, a wry grin on her face. She reached up and picked a glob of scrambled eggs out of his hair.

He grinned sheepishly. "I'm baby-sitting Kirk for Meghan today."

She nodded and swept past him. "That's why I'm

here. I saw Meghan leave earlier without Kirk and knew you must have pulled baby-sitting duty. How is that poor baby doing this morning?'' She shrugged out of her coat and threw it on the sofa and placed a paper sack she'd carried in next to it.

She went to where Kirk was seated on the floor amid a jumble of toys and scooped him up in her arms.

''Poor little boy,'' she said as she eyed the spots that dotted his face. ''I brought some oatmeal bath that should help soothe his skin.''

''Oatmeal? Does he eat it or bathe in it?''

Rose laughed. ''It's not like real oatmeal, but it's good for soothing an itch.''

''Great,'' Seth exclaimed, then frowned as he thought of bathing such a tiny creature.

Rose seemed to read his mind. ''How about I give him a quick bath while you fix him some lunch?''

''Sounds perfect,'' Seth said with relief. ''The bathroom is down the hallway. Towels are in the closet. Help yourself to whatever you need.''

''We'll be fine,'' Rose assured him. She grabbed the sack she'd brought with her, then disappeared down the hallway.

Seth went into the kitchen and prepared a small platter of sandwiches, then set the table for himself and Rose. He had a feeling an invitation to lunch would not be turned down by the old woman. And it was the least he could offer in return for her help.

A few minutes later she came into the kitchen,

carrying a freshly bathed Kirk in a clean pair of pajamas. Kirk offered Seth a weary smile.

"I think the bath helped make him more comfortable. Maybe once he eats his lunch, he'll take a nice nap for you," she said as she placed him in his high chair.

"You'll join us for lunch? It isn't exactly gourmet, just ham and cheese and tuna salad sandwiches." Seth handed Kirk a quarter of a sandwich, then gestured Rose to a chair.

"I'd rather eat tuna salad with somebody than steak or lobster by myself," Rose said as she sat at the table.

"You're a widow, right?" Seth asked.

Rose nodded. "I lost my Albert three years ago. We would have been married fifty years next month." For a moment Rose's broad face glowed with the warmth of memories...the memories that Seth knew came with years of loving somebody, of sharing one another's lives.

As Seth poured them each a soft drink, he remembered that he'd once looked forward to spending years with Meghan...had wanted to watch silvery highlights slowly etch into the strands of her hair, see the lines around her eyes deepen with shared life experience. He'd once wanted to grow old with her.

"Forty-seven years." Seth joined her at the table. "That's quite a long time. You were both very lucky."

"Luck had nothing to do with it," Rose scoffed and grabbed one of the tuna sandwiches. "Marriage is darn hard work and it has to be worked every day just like any other job if it's going to be successful.''

She tore off a piece of her sandwich and handed it to Kirk. ''So many people nowadays don't work at their relationships. Did you work at your marriage, Seth?''

''I put in a hundred and twenty percent, but it wasn't enough for my ex-wife.''

Rose shook her head. ''Too bad. So, are you planning on staying here through Christmas?'' she asked, changing the subject as she grabbed another half of a sandwich from the platter.

Seth shrugged. ''Meghan and I agreed that I should stay and watch Kirk for the rest of the week while she's at work.''

Seth had a feeling that after the next seven days, whether she'd gained the information he sought or not, he'd be out of here. But he would not leave here without some sort of agreement concerning Kirk. He was Kirk's father, and no matter Meghan's objections, he intended to be a father in every sense of the word.

Rose chewed her sandwich thoughtfully for a long moment. ''Are you going to tell me who you really are?''

Seth widened his eyes in surprise. ''Wha...what do you mean?''

''You didn't really think I'd swallow that cousin story did you?'' She eyed him with a touch of disgust. ''Tangled family tree, indeed.''

''Why don't you believe it?'' Seth countered.

"Because cousins don't look at each other the way you and Meghan do."

Seth forced a laugh to his lips. "What are you talking about?" he asked, trying to brazen it out.

Rose snorted. "I think you know exactly what I'm talking about. But I just can't figure it out." She took another bite of her sandwich and eyed him slyly. "I couldn't help but notice you're staying in the spare room."

"Couldn't help but notice?" Seth teased, knowing the only way she'd know that is if she looked into all the bedrooms.

Rose had the grace to blush. "Okay, so I'm a nosy old busybody and I peeked to see." She shrugged, then sighed mournfully. "I thought I smelled a romance going on, but apparently I was wrong." She dabbed her mouth with a paper napkin and sighed. "And I so want Meghan to be happy and in love."

Seth laughed and covered the old woman's hand with his. "Don't worry, Rose. I'm sure if you remain living next door to Meghan, eventually you'll get your wish to see her happy and in love with somebody." His words left a bad taste in his mouth as he thought of Meghan and David or some other man, living here together, loving each other and raising Kirk.

At that moment, Kirk began to fuss again. He rubbed his eyes with little fists and kicked at his chair in discontent.

"I think somebody is sleepy," Rose said. She

stood. "I'll just get out of here so you can get him down for a nap. Thanks so much for lunch, Steve."

Seth picked Kirk up and followed Rose to the living room where she pulled on her coat, then on to the front door. "Thanks Rose, for giving him a bath. Whatever you did seems to have helped a bit."

"It's the oatmeal bath. I left it in a bag in the bathroom." Rose smiled, a mischievous grin that made her look years younger. "I'm not giving up, you know. Something isn't what it seems around here, and I won't be happy until I get to the bottom of it."

Seth laughed once again as a burst of affection for the old busybody flowed through him. "I'm afraid you'll be sadly disappointed. There's no mystery here."

"We'll see," Rose replied, then wiggled her fingers and left.

Seth closed the door after her. "She'll never figure it out," he said to Kirk, who once again rubbed his eyes. Seth remembered the little tyke had been up and down all night. No wonder he was more than ready for a nap.

But Kirk didn't want to nap in his bed. When Seth took him into his room, he clung to Seth like a baby leech.

Seth sat in the rocking chair and tried to get him to fall asleep by rocking him, but with no success. Finally Seth returned to the living room and stretched out on the sofa, Kirk on his chest. Within minutes Kirk was sound asleep.

This was what Seth had hungered for from the moment he'd first laid eyes on Kirk…the opportunity to hold him close, smell the scent of him, feel his heartbeat against Seth's own.

Seth closed his eyes, his hand caressing Kirk's back. Was there a love any greater than that which flowed through him at this very moment? Had he ever felt this profound…protective love for any other human being in his life?

The answer came unbidden and filled him with a strange despair. Only once before…for Meghan.

Meghan got into her car and leaned her head wearily on the steering wheel. She couldn't remember the last time she'd been so tired.

All day long she'd felt the weight of Mark's suspicion. His gaze had lingered on her often, his brow wrinkled in deep thought. That, coupled with a near sleepless night had produced bone-weary exhaustion.

She'd battled with herself, trying to decide if she should come clean, tell him that Seth was hiding out in her house and that the work she'd tried to hide from Mark had been for him.

But she knew what would happen if she told Mark about Seth. Mark would contact Jonah, who in turn would send Seth back to the Condor Mountain Resort and Spa.

Meghan knew instinctively that if Seth was sent back there, the haunting shadows that had filled his eyes when he'd first arrived at her house would return. For the last couple of days those shadows had receded, but Meghan knew they weren't gone…they were only hiding inside him.

Seth needed the chance to find Simon, needed the hunt, the promise of revenge to keep his guilt at bay. Ultimately, she had known that to tell Mark meant to betray Seth. She hadn't been able to do that.

She raised her head and started the engine, wondering how Seth had fared with Kirk. She had a feeling he'd done just fine. Seth was nothing if not resourceful.

A half an hour later, she pulled up in front of the town house. For a moment she merely sat in the car and stared at the place she called home.

She'd bought the town house five years ago…long before she'd met Seth. She'd been twenty-six years old, had been making a good salary from the agency, and had decided it was time to build a nest for herself.

Although the town house with its four bedrooms had been far bigger than she'd needed, the price had been scandalously low due to the imminent divorce of the couple who owned it.

Besides, she'd bought it with dreams of the rooms being filled with children, hopes of a family's laughter and love permeating the entire place. Hopes and dreams that had been shattered by Seth's ultimate selfishness.

She got out of the car, tired of her thoughts, tired of the emotions that had been raging inside her for the past four days…ever since Seth had reentered her world.

The first thing that struck her when she entered the front door was the silence. "Hello?" she said softly. She took off her coat and hung it in the closet, then stepped into the living room and froze.

The room looked as if a natural disaster had occurred within the walls. A natural disaster named Kirk. Toys were everywhere. But the mess wasn't what captured her gaze.

Seth was on the sofa, Kirk on his chest, and both were sound asleep. Meghan's heart constricted at the sight of the two males…father and son. One who had held her heart, but had thrown it away, the other who would have her heart until the end of time.

She wasn't sure how long she stood there, watching Seth…watching Kirk. Their likeness in sleep awed her, and the obvious ease they found in each other's arms frightened her.

They belonged together. Every son needed his father in his life. Rose's words from the night before haunted her, and she resolutely shoved them away. Not all fathers were good for their children.

She blinked in surprise as she realized Seth's eyes were open and he was staring at her. "Hi," she said and sat down in the chair opposite the sofa.

"Hi. I didn't hear you come in," he said softly.

She swept her gaze around the room, then looked back at him once again. "Rough day?"

He grinned, a lazy gesture that lifted one corner of his mouth and created a ball of heat in the pit of Meghan's stomach. "A little rough, but we survived." His hand rubbed across Kirk's back. "Don't worry about the mess. I'll clean it up."

She shrugged, too tired to care. "You want me to take him and put him in bed?"

"Nah...he hasn't been asleep that long. He's been up and down since noon." He used one hand and shifted the pillow beneath his neck. "You look like hell."

"Gee, thanks." She laughed without humor. "You always were good at the sweet talk, Seth." She sighed and took off her glasses and set them on the table next to the chair.

"Rose came by earlier today. She brought some kind of oatmeal to bathe Kirk in. It seemed to help his itching."

"That was sweet of her." Meghan kicked off her high heels.

"Yeah, it was a mission of mercy, and a mission of snooping," Seth replied dryly.

Meghan eyed him curiously. "Snooping?"

He rubbed Kirk's back as the little boy stirred, then grew silent again. "She didn't buy the cousin story and she's certain there's some sort of mystery here."

"Oh, terrific." Meghan rubbed her forehead wearily. "I'm too tired to think about it at the moment."

"Why don't you go in and take a nap."

A nap sounded wonderful. "I should do something about dinner," she replied without conviction.

"We can order a pizza or something later," he replied. "Go on, Meg...a nap will do you wonders."

His use of the diminutive of her name nearly undid her. The last time he'd called her Meg they had been making love. The last time he had called her Meg, she'd thought eternity was theirs.

"Maybe I will stretch out for just a little while." She stood, aware that her tiredness had her emotions far too close to the surface.

"I'll wake you when the pizza gets here," Seth said.

She nodded and headed for her room. Once there, she stripped off her dress and hose and climbed beneath the blankets clad in her slip and underclothes.

"Every boy needs his father in his life." Rose's voice filled her head. Meghan closed her eyes, wondering what she was going to do about Seth and Kirk.

She'd believed in her heart she'd made the right choice when she'd called Seth to tell her she was pregnant and that she wanted him to stay out of their lives.

She rolled over on her stomach, her mind racing back in time...back to her own childhood. She could still remember the feel of her mother's hands gripping hers in desperation.

"What will we do, Meghan? What will we do if something happens to your daddy?" Her mother's grip had become painfully tight, but not as painful as the fear that had clutched Meghan's heart. "I'll die...if anything happens to him, I'll just die."

And if her father died...and her mother died... what would happen to Meghan?

She shoved the memories aside, not wanting to

remember the horror of those days...those nights with her mother. Her childhood had been one of fear and she absolutely refused to allow that same kind of fear to rule Kirk's life. Unless Seth quit his job with the agency, she would not allow him to be a part of his son's life.

She drew a deep breath as sleep reached out to her, filling her head with fuzzy, dreamlike images. And in those images Seth was calling her Meg, and kissing her lips and caressing her skin and loving her. And she knew she was dreaming, because she didn't want him to stop...but wanted him to go on loving her forever.

Kirk awoke soon after Meghan disappeared into her bedroom. To Seth's relief, he seemed more like himself and entertained himself with the wooden set of blocks while Seth picked up the rest of the toys and put them away in the nursery.

When he had the living room back in order, he carried Kirk into the kitchen and opened up several jars of toddler food he found in the cabinet. As they warmed in the microwave, Kirk banged on his tray impatiently.

"Just a minute, kiddo. Daddy is working as fast as he can," Seth said.

He transferred the food onto Kirk's plastic plate, then placed the food before him and sat down at the table next to him. "Okay buddy, dig in."

Kirk grinned, then reached out and grabbed Seth's nose. "Daddy," he said.

For a long moment, Seth remained utterly still, rich emotion sweeping through him. For the first time he recognized the joy of having a child…this child calling him Daddy.

"Yeah, I'm your daddy," he replied.

Kirk nodded and released his nose, then focused on the meal before him.

Seth watched him eat, loving him…laughing as Kirk missed his mouth with his spoon, smearing applesauce and macaroni across his plump cheeks.

He and Meghan needed to talk. Every day brought her closer to finding the information he needed, every day brought him closer to leaving, but he couldn't leave without the issue of Kirk being settled between them.

*What do you know about being a father?* A tiny voice whispered in the back of his head. *You didn't even have a relationship with your own father.*

Seth frowned, a whisper of fear dancing through him as he thought of his old man. Seth and his father had never bonded in any significant way. In the darkest reaches of his mind, Seth wondered if he'd tried a little harder, worked more diligently, would he have been able to save his father's life?

He shoved these thoughts away. What was past…was past. His father was dead and nothing would bring him back. It had nothing to do with the present or Seth's future. It had simply been a tragedy in time…a single memory that Seth refused to allow to bleed into any other area of his life.

After feeding Kirk, Seth took him into the bathroom and gave him an oatmeal bath, then changed his diaper and clothes and played with him for a while. By that time Kirk was rubbing his eyes, indicating sleep would come soon.

By eight-thirty, Kirk was sound asleep in his crib and Seth paced the living room, wondering if he should go ahead and order pizza. Would Meghan want him to wake her?

He went down the hallway to her bedroom door. Surely she'd want to eat something. Surely she wouldn't want to nap so long that she'd awaken at some ungodly hour of the morning unable to go back to sleep.

He turned the knob and quietly opened the door. The room was near dark with the falling of night outside, but the spill of the night-light in the outlet near the bed painted Meghan in golden hues.

She was on her stomach, her hair a wild tangle of red curls. He could tell she slept soundly by the deepness, the evenness of her breathing.

Her shoulders were exposed, displaying a wealth of freckles...like cream with a sprinkle of nutmeg. Seth felt a tightening in his groin as a wave of pure desire swept through him.

He fought against it, knowing desire had no place in his current situation with Meghan. They were separate...divorced, without hope for any future together. And yet, no matter how he tried to resist, his body refused to be cooled.

"Meghan," he said softly.

She didn't stir.

And suddenly he found himself right next to the bed, so close to her if he wanted he could reach out his hand and touch those charming freckles that seemed to taunt him. And he wanted.

He eased down next to her on the bed and placed his hand on her shoulder, felt the heat that radiated from her skin…a heat that stoked the flames inside him.

She stirred, but didn't turn around, didn't open her eyes. Seth placed his other hand on her other shoulder and began to massage the sweet-scented, soft skin.

"Hmm," she moaned with pleasure. The sexy sound of that moan roared in Seth's head and he fought the impulse to press his lips against her skin.

The white straps of her slip and bra looked erotically sexy against her skin, but quickly became irritations as Seth yearned to run his hands unencumbered across her entire back.

He pulled the blankets down to her waist and massaged across the small of her back, the silky slip material warming beneath his touch. She moaned again and he wanted to rip the blankets off the bed, pull her slip over her head, remove her bra and panties, and lose himself in her.

"Seth." Her voice sliced through the fog that threatened to overwhelm him. He drew his hands back, his breath catching painfully in his chest as he waited to see if she intended to send him away.

She turned over on her back. Her eyes were the deep green of summer…hot and radiant. "Seth…

what are you doing?'' Her voice was a husky whisper that shot rivulets of fire through him.

''I'm not sure,'' he replied. ''And I'm not sure I can stop.''

She drew a deep breath, her breasts rising and falling beneath the lacy slip. ''Then heaven help us both...because I don't want you to stop.''

# Chapter 10

When he'd first touched her, Meghan had believed it to be part of her dream. She'd been dreaming of Seth and in her dream they'd been making love. However, as his touch had lingered, she'd realized it was real. No dream could be so sweet and vivid. No dream could evoke such heat inside her like she felt at the moment. The last of her sleep fell away as reality sank in.

Seth was on her bed, touching her with fingers of fire and she didn't want the contact to stop.

"Kirk?" she asked, suddenly tensing as she thought of her son.

"Asleep."

She relaxed at his single word reply.

As he pulled his shirt over his head, his eyes green

pools of hunger, there was no more room for thought in her head. She had no intention of calling a halt to the lovemaking she knew was about to occur.

It had been inevitable. From the instant he'd shown up on her front porch, this moment had been as inevitable as the fall of night in the evenings...as the rise of the sun in the morning.

She didn't stop to wonder why he wanted her now, when he hadn't wanted her before. At the moment it didn't matter. She only knew she wanted him as she never had before.

With his shirt off, he reached for her, and she sat up and went willingly into his arms. His mouth possessed hers with an urgency, a wildness that tore through her to her very core.

He tangled his hands in her hair, drawing her closer...closer still, until her slip-covered breasts were pulled tight against his bare chest. He slid one hand behind her head, as if to hold her steady while his mouth plundered hers.

She touched his shoulders first, running her hands across the taut muscles, then wrapped her arms around him, giving her hands free rein to play across his broad back.

Any lingering sleepiness that might have existed in her fell away as she slid into his kiss. The taste of him brought her triumphantly to life, filling her with a joy that surged through her blood, sang in her veins.

A moan released itself from her as his lips left hers

and instead blazed a trail of fire down her jawline and into the hollow of her throat.

"Meg…Meg…sweet Meg," he murmured, his breath hot against her neck.

"Seth," she sighed, loving the sound, the feel of his name on her lips.

His hands left her hair and instead caressed down her back and she arched like a cat beneath a stroking hand.

She wasn't sure who pushed the blankets aside, Seth or her. In any case, the bedspread fell to the floor and the sheet was shoved down at their feet.

He kissed her shoulders, then pushed the straps of her slip and bra off her shoulders in an effort to be rid of them.

She aided him, eager to feel her bare flesh against his. She reached down and grabbed the bottom of the slip and pulled it off over her head. Reaching behind her for the clasp of her bra, she watched as he stood at the side of the bed and took off his jeans.

Clad only in a pair of briefs, his desire was more than evident. Still he stood, watching as she unclasped her bra and took it off. "You are so beautiful," he said, his voice a low, near-guttural growl.

And then he was back on the bed with her, his arms surrounding her as his lips once again found hers. Her tongue slid over his lips and he moaned, a moan that seemed to find its origin in his very soul.

They were flesh to flesh, the only barrier the underpants they both wore. Seth moved so he was half over the top of her, his mouth once again tasting the skin of her neck, nipping lightly over her collarbones.

When his mouth found the peak of one breast, Meghan arched with pleasure. His tongue played across her nipple and shuddering sensations of response soared through her.

She twisted her hands in his hair, loving the texture of the silken strands around her fingers. Her breath caught in her throat as his mouth left her breasts and he licked lightly down the flat of her stomach.

He paused at the lacy edge of her panties and Meghan wondered if it were possible for a heart to explode. Then, his lips returned the way they had come, warming her stomach and once again finding the tip of her breasts.

"Seth...make love to me," she cried, unable to stand the tension that coiled inside her.

He raised his head and looked at her, his eyes filled with a need that reverberated inside Meghan. "Not yet." His voice was a soft promise of pleasure to come and Meghan shivered with the heat of that promise.

He held her gaze as his hand lazily traced the waistband of her panties, then trailed down her hips to caress her inner thighs, never touching where she needed to be touched most.

Teasing. He'd always loved to tease her, start her on fire until she was nearly consumed. Then, and only then, would he take her.

"Did I tell you that you're beautiful," he asked, his breath a whisper of heat against her face.

"You did, but you can tell me again and again," she returned breathlessly.

"You are the most beautiful woman I've ever known," he said.

"And you're beautiful, too," she replied. It was true. Seth, with the glow of the night-light painting his bold features, looked beautiful and strong and utterly masculine.

He stroked a hand down her cheek and pressed his lips against hers. And in this kiss...so tender...so soft, she realized she had never stopped loving Seth.

Despite their divorce, in spite of their angry recriminations, and the bitterness of their parting, he was still in her heart. She loved him more than ever.

With this knowledge came the awareness that she should stop this madness before they actually made love, that in making love to Seth again, he would only manage to burrow further...deeper into her heart than he already was.

But she didn't want to listen to the wisdom, didn't want to think about all the reasons why this might not be a good idea.

For now...for this very moment in time, it was right. And she could no more call a halt to it than stop breathing.

As he broke the soft kiss, his hand moved down the length of her body and found the center of her heat, rubbing her gently through the silky fabric of her panties.

Meghan returned the caress, stroking his hips, touching the smooth skin of his inner thigh, teasing him as he had teased her only moments before.

His response was explosive. He tore off his briefs, then removed her panties, then eased himself between her legs and deep within her.

For a moment neither of them moved. It was as if not only their bodies were intimately entwined, but also their hearts, their souls, leaving nothing left to do but exist in the moment, and in each other.

It was he who moved first...a slight shifting of his hips that created hot pleasure to sear through her. He gazed down at her, his eyes making love to her as effectively as his body.

As he moved again, Meghan closed her eyes and gave herself to the sheer pleasure of loving Seth.

Seth wanted slow. He wanted to love her forever, to make each and every exquisite sensation last endless minutes...hours. But his eager body refused to listen to his heart's desire, wanting...needing to move with a frantic pace all its own.

She was softness and warmth and fulfillment and it wasn't just physical pleasure that filled him, but emotional pleasure as well. They moved together, like one entity, their sighs and gasps echoing softly in the room.

Slow. *Slow.* Seth told himself, but he moved faster and faster with her...in her...felt himself swept up in a vortex of sensation that sent him higher and higher.

She climbed, too. Arching against him, meeting him thrust for thrust. Her fingers gripped his shoulders, nails biting slightly into his skin. She whispered his name over and over again, like a sweet song of joy with no other words.

And he knew when she reached her peak, felt her body tense, then shudder and at the same time, he went over the edge, crying out her name as if it were the answer to her song.

Moments later, they lay in each other's arms. Their breathing had returned to normal, their bodies had cooled, but there was a fragile peace between them that formed an intimate connection that had nothing to do with their lovemaking.

For the moment, there was no bitter past between them, no future to worry about…just now, with each other. "What time is it?" Meghan asked.

Seth turned his head to see her alarm clock. "Nine-thirty," he replied.

"Did Kirk eat supper?"

"Yeah, I gave him a couple jars of stuff I found in the pantry. I put him in bed about eight-thirty and he fell right to sleep."

She snuggled closer to him. "Seth?"

"Yeah?" He used one hand to caress the silky softness of her hair.

"Why did you send me away the other night? The night when I woke you from your nightmare…why did you say those things to make me mad?"

Seth sighed and closed his eyes, his fingers still

dancing in the silky strands of hair. "I was trying to keep what just happened from happening."

"You didn't want to make love to me that night?"

He heard the slight hurt in her voice and opened his eyes. Raising up on one elbow, he stared down at her. With her hair all tangled and her lips still swollen slightly from his kisses, she nearly took his breath away.

"I was crazy with wanting you that night." He remembered how, when she'd left the room, his fingers still tingled from touching her, his mouth burned from her kisses, and his stomach ached with need.

Her eyes flared at his words. She raised a hand and placed the palm of it against his cheek. "I felt the same way, too. So...why did you send me away?"

He sighed, raked a hand through his hair, then lay back down and stared at the ceiling. "Because I knew this might complicate things between us."

"So, what changed tonight?"

He went back to stroking her hair, remembering that moment when he'd walked into her room and seen her in bed. "The moment I saw you here, your hair all wild and curly against the pillow, your shoulders peeking out from the blankets, I knew I had to touch you. And after I touched you, I knew I had to kiss you, and after I kissed you, I knew I had to make love to you." The words spilled from him, impossible to halt.

"Actually, the day I first arrived, when I saw you get out of the car, I knew I wanted to make love to you again. And each day I've been here, that want has grown stronger and stronger. I guess tonight I had no control, I couldn't stop myself.''

This time it was she who raised herself up on one elbow and gazed at him. ''But this changes nothing between us.'' It wasn't as much a question as a statement of fact. ''If you were somehow afraid that I'd mistaken this for a promise for the future, you're wrong.''

She bit her bottom lip, her eyes as luminous as he'd ever seen them. ''I mean, we both know sex never solved anything for us, only this time there is nothing to solve. We're divorced. We've each moved on with our lives. Fate just gave us a second chance to find a little pleasure with each other.''

He wanted to protest the cool rationale of her words, but wasn't sure what there was to protest. She was right. This changed nothing between them. Their lives were separate by choice, by her choice. She hadn't loved him for the man he was…only the man she'd wanted to make him.

This thought cooled any residual desire that might have reawakened and better prepared him for the conversation he knew they had to have. He would never again have Meghan in his life, but he could at least have his son.

''Meghan, some things have changed,'' he began.

She tensed and pulled the sheet up to cover her nakedness, as if expecting something unpleasant. ''What do you mean?''

''I mean we need to talk about Kirk…and me.''

In one single, graceful movement, she left the bed. "There's nothing to talk about," she replied as she pulled on her robe and belted it at her waist.

"Yes, there is…where are you going?" he asked as she headed for the door.

"To get something to eat. I'm starving." She disappeared down the hallway.

Seth scrambled from the bed and grabbed his clothes. They were going to have this conversation now, he thought with grim determination as he dressed.

By the time he got to the kitchen, she stood in front of the refrigerator, eyeing the contents with obvious distaste. "I thought you were going to order pizza," she said as she slammed the refrigerator door and opened the freezer.

"I was. I got sidetracked."

She pulled a frozen pizza from the freezer, then set the oven temperature. "Then, I guess it's frozen for tonight." She went to the cabinet that held the plates. She turned to him and smiled…a forced smile that didn't reach her eyes. "Are you eating with me?"

He shook his head, knowing she was attempting to distract him. "Meghan, we can talk about it tonight, or we can talk about it tomorrow, but sooner or later, we have to deal with it."

She unwrapped the pizza, her forehead wrinkled with a frown. "As far as I'm concerned, there is nothing to discuss." She turned away from him, but not before he saw a shimmer of fear in the depths of her eyes.

The fear confused him. "Meghan." He stood and watched as she put the pizza into the oven. When she was finished, he advanced toward her, his hands out in entreaty. "I don't want to fight, Meghan."

"Good, on that we both agree." She stepped around him and went back to the refrigerator for a cold can of soda.

"I would never do anything to hurt you or Kirk, and I don't want to take him away from you. I just want to share custody of him." He finally said the words that had been forming inside him for days, words he knew she'd been dreading to hear.

"Why do we have to talk about this now?" she asked, pain lacing her voice. "We just made love. My body still feels the imprint of yours...what we shared was beautiful and wonderful. Why are you trying to ruin it? Why are you intentionally picking a fight with me at this moment?"

"I'm not intentionally picking a fight," he protested, although deep in his heart, he knew that's exactly what he was doing. He knew this conversation would be difficult, that she'd fight with him on this particular topic. So, why, indeed, did he feel the need to discuss it right now at this moment?

The answer came to him, surprising him. He had intentionally chosen this moment to discuss the issue of Kirk in order to distance himself from what they had just shared in the bedroom.

His skin still smelled of her, his body still retained

the warmth from hers, and his heart...his heart had been touched by her in a way that frightened him. He'd brought up the topic of Kirk because he felt weak and vulnerable, and he knew in fighting with her, he'd gain back his equilibrium.

But, now...looking at her...seeing the pain he was causing her, he felt even more weak and small. "Okay," he relented. "We won't discuss it any further tonight."

"Thank you," she said softly and the smile she gave him, so warm and grateful, once again sent him reeling off balance.

# *Chapter 11*

Meghan pulled off her glasses and rubbed her eyes wearily, then put them back on and gazed at her watch. In another hour she could go home.

Tomorrow was Christmas and her life had never been so muddled and confusing. Kirk's chicken pox marks were beginning to scab over and he was feeling much better. He and Seth had become inseparable buddies over the past seven days.

Seeing them together each evening, watching the bonds of love grow stronger was a particular kind of agony for Meghan.

She had a fierce desire to protect her son, and yet worried that in protecting him, she'd ultimately deprive him.

Seth hadn't brought up the issue of sharing cus-

tody again since the night that they'd made love, and
for that she was grateful. She didn't know what to
do, knew her head told her to get him out of both
her life and Kirk's, but her heart was so torn.

David had called her the day before, and the moment she'd heard his voice, she knew she had to tell
him there was nothing—would never be anything—
between them.

It was impossible to find a new love when an old
love was sleeping in the room next door. Impossible
to allow a new man into her heart when Seth already
filled it so completely.

"Meghan."

Mark's voice pulled her from her thoughts and she
gazed at her co-worker. She'd been shocked when
she'd arrived that morning to find Mark at work. He
rarely worked on Sundays. Tension had ripped
through the office for the past six days, the tense aura
of suspicion. Meghan didn't know how to dispel it
without telling Mark about Seth, but she hated knowing that Mark had grown distrustful of her.

"Can I talk to you for a minute before you get
ready to knock off for the holidays?"

"Of course," she replied. She pushed away from
her desk and turned her chair to face his.

Mark reached for one of the sugar cookies a client
had brought in and Meghan tensed. The conversation
was not going to be pleasant, if Mark needed to sustain himself with sugar.

He raked a hand through his hair and studied her

for a long moment, silently munching on the cookie until it was gone. "I'm worried sick about you."

She eyed him in surprise. "Why?"

"You're hiding something. You've been strange for the past week or so....secretive...furtive." He reached for another cookie, a deep frown marring his normally placid, pleasant features. "Now, I did some checking and I know you don't seem to be suffering any kind of financial crunch."

"What?" Meghan glared at him in outrage. "What do you mean, you did some checking?"

A slight blush stained Mark's cheeks. "You aren't the only one around here with a few computer skills."

"You got into my financial records? How dare you!" Anger swept through Meghan. "I've worked with you for years. I thought we were friends." She punched off her computer as if she were punching out Mark's eyes.

"We are friends," Mark protested. "That's why I haven't gone to Jonah yet with my suspicions."

"What suspicions?" Meghan stood and stalked to the closet. She grabbed a bottle of spray cleaner and a clean cloth, then returned to her desk.

"My suspicions that you're selling out."

"Oh, Mark, you couldn't be more wrong." Meghan set the cleaning supplies on her desk and ran a weary hand through her hair. "You know me, Mark. I would never do anything to jeopardize the agency. I'm as committed to SPEAR as any field agent, any other worker in the agency."

Mark stood and grabbed her hands. "Then, for God's sake, please tell me what's going on with you. Meghan, please talk to me."

Suddenly Meghan wanted...*needed* to talk to somebody. She pulled her hands from his and gestured him back to his chair. "You'd better sit down."

"Oh no, it's worse than I thought," Mark said mournfully.

"It's nothing like what you thought," Meghan returned. She sank onto her chair. "Seth is at my house. He's been there since he left the Condor Mountain Resort."

Mark's eyes widened in shocked surprise. "Wow...in a million years I would have never guessed that."

"No, you preferred to guess that I was a traitor," Meghan replied dryly.

Mark looked chagrined. "Sorry, but I didn't know what else to think. You've been showing up here early, sneaking time at the computer on things you won't let me see. You've been distracted and preoccupied." Mark shrugged. "Hey, I can't help it. I've been trained to be suspicious."

Meghan grinned at him. "It's okay. You're forgiven. I'm just grateful you decided to confront me before going to Jonah with your suspicions."

"So, what's going on with Seth?"

*I've fallen in love all over again with him.* The words exploded in Meghan's mind, filling her with a curious mixture of joy and grief. But she knew that wasn't what Mark wanted to hear.

"When he arrived at my place, he was filled with guilt over the L.A. sting operation. He asked me if he could stay with me while I try to find the whereabouts of the drugs Simon stole."

"Then he'll know where Simon is. And that explains what you've been doing here."

Meghan nodded. "I tried to turn him away, Mark. I told him he needed to go back to the Condor, that he couldn't take responsibility for the busted sting operation, but he wouldn't listen."

"And so now he's a lone, loose cannon ready to go off?"

Meghan smiled. "Not exactly. Seth is guilt-ridden and maybe a little obsessed with finding Simon, but he's not stupid enough to take Simon on all alone. I'm sure if and when he discovers where Simon is, he'll contact Jonah and set up some sort of operation."

"Wow, I still can't believe Seth has been in your house for the past week. How has that been?" Mark raised his eyebrows, looking like a mischievous young boy. "Any sparks reborn between the two of you?"

To Meghan's horror, she burst into tears. She wasn't sure who the tears surprised more, Mark or herself. All she knew was the tension, the pressure, the utter agony of loving Seth spilled from her in huge gulping sobs.

"Gosh, Meghan, I'm sorry. I'm so sorry I asked," Mark exclaimed.

She laughed through her tears as she saw the expression on Mark's face...an expression of helpless terror. He raced to the water cooler and got a paper cup of water, then returned to her and held it out.

"Here...drink this."

She took a swallow of the water and struggled for control. Drawing several deep breaths, she withdrew a handful of tissues from her purse and swiped at her tears. "I'm sorry," she said. "I didn't mean for that to happen."

"I didn't mean to make that happen," Mark said.

She offered him a watery smile. "You didn't." The smile fell away beneath the weight of her inner turmoil. "Oh Mark, I've gone and done a dumb thing. I've fallen back in love with my ex-husband."

Mark emitted a soft, deep whistle. "And what does Seth think about this?"

"Who knows? And in any case, what difference does it make? The problems that drove us apart will always stand between us." She dabbed at her eyes once again, wondering how it was possible for a broken heart to break all over again? "There's absolutely no future for me and Seth." She said the last words with a note of finality.

"I'm sorry, Meghan. I always thought you and Seth were great together. I don't know what your problems were before, but it's too bad they can't be solved."

*Too bad they can't be solved. You and Seth were great together.* Mark's words echoed in Meghan's head as she drove home a little while later.

She didn't know if Seth still loved her or not. In

the time he'd been in her home, he'd said nothing to indicate that he did. But, even if he did love her, she couldn't live with the knowledge that each time he walked out the front door, he might be killed or maimed in the line of duty.

She'd lived that particular fear all through her childhood years. She refused to relive it through her marriage.

But for the past six days, she'd felt almost like she and Seth were reliving their marriage. Although they had not made love again, their evenings had been spent like many married couples, playing with their son and enjoying one another's company.

If only things could be like that forever, she thought as she drove home. If only Seth would stay forever. But she knew that wasn't possible. The moment she found the information he sought, he'd be off and running on a mission that would put his life at risk.

And she would once again be left alone to pick up the pieces of her life. This time she'd move forward with her life and never again look back, never again allow Seth entry into her heart.

For now, he had once again become firmly lodged in her heart and she knew heartache was inevitable, but that didn't make it easier for her to stop loving Seth.

Him being here for the holiday was like a perverse gift from fate, a second chance to get it wrong. But she also knew the memories of this time with Seth and Kirk would warm her on many cold, lonely nights to come.

Just enjoy the moment, she told herself as she got out of her car. Don't think about tomorrow or yesterday, just enjoy having Seth in your life for this moment in time.

"Hello?" she called out as she stepped into the house.

"We're in here," Seth yelled from the kitchen.

She hung up her coat, dropped her purse by the hall closet, then walked into the kitchen to see Kirk in his high chair, Seth at the stove, and a glass of wine poured and waiting for her.

"Mama!" Kirk greeted her with a big smile and stretched out his arms for a hug.

She complied, kissing Kirk on his forehead and giving him a tight squeeze. "How's my baby today?"

"I'm just fine," Seth replied with an easy grin that warmed Meghan to her toes.

"I was talking about my other baby," she replied dryly. She kicked off her shoes and sank down at the table, her fingers curling around the glass of wine.

"I think he's feeling much better. He was into everything today." Seth removed a pan of soup from the burner. "We're having soup and sandwiches for dinner."

"Sounds marvelous," Meghan replied. "Can I do anything to help?"

"No, I've got it under control." He flashed her

that smile that warmed her throughout. "Just sit and relax and give me a little adult conversation."

She laughed. "You sound like a lonely, frustrated housewife."

"I'll tell you what. Cooking and cleaning and taking care of a fourteen-month-old is damn hard work. I don't know how you've managed to do it all alone."

Meghan shrugged, trying not the remember all the nights she'd longed for somebody to hold her close, rub her back, offer comfort and companionship. "You do what you have to do."

She watched as Seth pulled the sandwich makings from the refrigerator. As she sipped her wine, she drank in his presence.

He made the sandwiches with an efficiency of movement, maneuvering the kitchen with familiarity. Wearing a burgundy sweater and a pair of jeans, he looked utterly masculine and overwhelmingly attractive.

"Mama," Kirk said and pointed to her with a smile. "Daddy," he added, then pointed at Seth.

"Yeah buddy, I'm right here," Seth answered absently.

A shock rippled through Meghan. When had Kirk begun calling Seth daddy? It was obvious this was not the first time by Seth's reaction. And why shouldn't Kirk call him daddy? Seth was Kirk's father and nothing in the world would ever change that fact.

"Tell me about your day," Seth said as he placed the plate of sandwiches on the table.

Meghan handed Kirk a cracker. "There isn't much to tell. We had barbecue for lunch and I told Mark you were here." She held her breath, waiting for his reaction.

He paused, soup ladle in the air and stared at her in disbelief. "You're joking."

"No, I'm not." Meghan finished the last of her wine. "Seth, you put me in a difficult position." She hurried to explain in an attempt to ward off Seth's anger. "Mark was growing more and more suspicious of me. He thought I was selling out to another agency…another government. I had to tell him the truth."

He set the soup ladle down and walked over to where she sat. She steeled herself for an explosion, but instead he placed his hands gently on her shoulders, his gaze warm as it lingered on her.

"I never considered how difficult things might get for you with Mark." He leaned down and kissed her gently…sweetly on the forehead. Heat soared through her at the touch of his lips against her skin. "I'm sorry for putting you in that position," he said, then released her and stepped back to the stove.

"Mark has promised he won't tell anyone, including Jonah," she said, and tried to ignore how much she wanted to be in Seth's arms. "In fact, he's offered to help in the search for the drugs."

Seth served the soup and placed the bowls on the table. "I guess two experts are better than one." He joined her at the table. "As soon as we finish eating, I've got to run out for a few minutes."

She looked at him in surprise. "Run out? I thought you were in hiding here."

"I am, but something has come up that I have to do." He reached for a handful of crackers and crumbled them into his soup.

"Seth, what could be so important that you'd risk going out and having somebody see you?" she asked worriedly.

He grinned, that wonderful, lazy, sexy grin that created a ball of warmth in the pit of her stomach. "In case you've forgotten, it's Christmas Eve. As one of Santa's appointed elves, there are a few things I need to do to make certain the jolly old man's trip around the world goes smoothly."

"I think you're suffering holiday delusion," Meghan retorted with a laugh.

"Not true," he protested. "I'm sure you're not aware of this, but every Christmas Eve, I don green tights and an elve's hat and make sure the skyway is clear for Santa's deliveries."

Meghan laughed again, trying to imagine her handsome husband in a pair of green tights and an elve's hat. Her laughter faded as she realized she'd thought of Seth as her husband, not an ex-husband who would be gone when the next assignment called.

Seth flipped the coat collar up around his neck, then grabbed the stocking cap Meghan held out to him. He pulled the cap on his head, then turned to face her. "Would you recognize me?"

"In a heartbeat," she replied. "But there will be a mob out there, so I think you'll be okay." She reached and tucked a strand of his hair up beneath the cap. "You need a haircut."

"You always tell me that." Seth fought the desire to wrap his arms around her and pull her tight against him. All he could think about was making love to her again.

She was like a virus, infecting him through and through and like most viruses, there didn't seem to be a cure.

Too much time alone...too much time cooped up in the house, he thought as he headed out the door. He wasn't accustomed to having so much time to be introspective, wasn't used to being in a place that breathed of Meghan.

He drew a deep breath of the cold, evening air and headed for Meghan's car. Once in the car, he again felt himself surrounded by her presence. Her scent lingered in the air and filled him with a frustrating need.

He headed toward the nearest shopping mall, his thoughts remaining on Meghan. He'd hoped that in making love to her one last time, he'd finally, irrevocably get her out of his system.

However, instead, making love to her had reawakened the love he felt for her, a love that had never really died, but rather had just gone deep into his heart where it couldn't hurt him anymore.

As he pulled into the packed parking lot of the mall, he shoved these disturbing emotions back deep inside him, refusing to entertain them any further. It was a hopeless situation and he'd rather focus on the immediate problem... Christmas presents for both Meghan and Kirk.

Meghan's prediction was correct. The mall was jammed with last minute shoppers like himself; harried parents looking for that desired toy, worried husbands seeking redemption in the perfect gift, and irritable salesclerks who had obviously had enough of the retail madness.

Seth joined in the fracas, going from store to store, up and down aisles, seeking what, he wasn't sure. He only knew he'd know it when he found it.

He was intensely aware that this would be his first gift to Kirk and probably his last to Meghan. He wanted both to be perfect.

It took him nearly two hours to complete the job. Finally, satisfied with his purchases, he headed toward the nearest mall exit.

"Steve! Yoo-hoo."

The familiar voice stopped him in his tracks. He turned to see Rose hurrying toward him. "Hi, Rose. What are you doing here on the worse shopping night of the year?"

"Not shopping," she said with a cheerful laugh. "I always come to the mall on Christmas Eve." She pointed to a sandwich shop. "I sit in there and have a cup of coffee and watch the shoppers."

A wave of compassion struck Seth for the old

woman who had no family. He had a feeling the holiday season was difficult for her and for the first time he wondered how difficult last Christmas had been for Meghan who'd been alone with a two-month-old baby. "Why don't you come over in the morning and share a cup of coffee with us?" he offered.

"I might just do that," she said with a wide smile. "Now, what have you got in those bags? Presents for Meghan and Kirk?" She eyed his shopping bags curiously.

"Yeah, I figured I'd better pick up something for them or she'll kick me out."

"Let me see what you bought for them." Rose's eyes sparkled and Seth realized she was a woman who could gain pleasure by other people's gifts.

Still he hesitated showing her what he'd bought. Showing her Kirk's present would be no problem. However, Meghan's gift was a whole different story. "I got Kirk a little computer that's supposed to teach him his alphabet and colors and shapes," he said, hoping that satisfied her.

"That sounds darling." She gestured for him to open the bag. "Show me."

Seth took the fancy-boxed toy out of the sack and showed it to her. "Ah, so many buttons and keys...he'll love it, I'm sure." She watched him put the toy back in the bag, then waited expectantly. "And for Meghan?" she finally asked.

Seth waved one hand dismissively. "I just got her something to wear," he said.

"A sweater? A dress?" Rose stepped closer to him, sensing intrigue.

"Not exactly," Seth stalled, then realized such a technique was like waving fresh meat in front of a starving dog. With a deep sigh of reluctance, he showed Rose what he'd bought Meghan, aware that in doing so he was feeding her suspicions.

"Cousins, indeed," she scoffed when he'd put the item back in the bag. The smile that had decorated her face since she'd stopped him fell away, replaced by a steely sternness that surprised Seth.

She drew a deep breath and stared him straight in the eyes. "I don't know who you are, or what you're doing staying in Meghan's house. But I'm begging you, don't hurt that girl. She's been through a lot and was devastated when her husband left her. She doesn't need any more pain in her life."

"I know," Seth replied softly. "And it's not my intention to bring her any more pain."

"Good." Rose's smile returned. "Now, you'd better get home and get those wrapped. Maybe I'll see you in the morning for a cup of coffee." With a wiggle of several fingers, Rose left and headed in the direction of the sandwich shop.

Seth watched her settle into a chair, then he turned and left the mall. He felt as if he'd swallowed a lead weight as he thought of his words to Rose. He didn't want to hurt Meghan but he had a feeling it was too late.

In the end, they seemed destined to love one another…and hurt one another.

## Chapter 12

"Merry Christmas!"

The deep, familiar voice pierced through Meghan's sleep and pulled her from sweet dreams. She opened her eyes to see Seth standing next to her bed, a smiling Kirk in his arms.

"Mama," Kirk said, then laughed with delight as Seth dropped him in the center of the bed. Seth stretched out next to him, a wide grin on his face.

"Merry Christmas," Meghan replied, her heart warmed by the thought of her bed filled with the men she loved most in the world.

"It snowed all night long," Seth said. "Kirk wants to go outside and build a snowman."

"He does?" Meghan reached for her glasses on the nightstand, then propped herself up on an elbow facing Kirk and Seth. "He told you that?"

"He did. When I was changing his diaper and dressing him, he told me he wanted his mommy and daddy to take him outside to play in the snow."

"Mommy. Daddy." Kirk echoed, then laughed.

Meghan embraced the moment, and the sight of them in her heart. Seth looked particularly handsome clad in a pair of jeans and a festive red sweater. His hair was slightly disheveled and his eyes sparkled merrily.

"Then I guess I'd better get up and get dressed for some fun in the snow," Meghan replied.

Seth smiled again, a boyish grin that weakened Meghan's knees and made her grateful she wasn't standing. "Come on, Kirk." Seth stood and scooped the little boy up in his arms. "Let's get out of here so Mommy can get dressed, then your daddy is going to show you how to make the best snowman in the world."

Minutes later Meghan rejoined Seth and Kirk in the hallway, where Seth was wrestling Kirk into his snowsuit. "This thing must have been designed by a sadist," he said as he maneuvered Kirk's legs into the suit. "There," he exclaimed triumphantly as he successfully zipped up the bright blue suit.

He lifted Kirk up and set him on his feet, then turned to Meghan. "Are you sure you'll be warm enough?" he asked as he took in her red sweat suit.

"I'll be fine." She pulled her coat from the closet and buttoned it up, then added a hat, scarf and gloves. As she readied herself, Seth slid his coat and hat on and together the three of them walked out into the wintry wonderland.

It was still snowing big, fat flakes against a gray sky. There was a good five or six inches already on the ground. Kirk took a tentative step, then reached out a hand to Seth.

"It's snow, buddy," Seth explained.

"No," Kirk said in an attempt to repeat.

Meghan watched father and son, and her heart expanded to fill her chest. At the same time, confusing thoughts whirled through her head.

How could she keep this man from his son? His love for Kirk was so overwhelmingly obvious. How could she deny Kirk the pleasure of having Seth in his life?

She had never been so torn over an issue before. Inviting Seth into Kirk's life on a permanent basis was not without its negative side. What she had to decide was if the positive outweighed the negative.

"Come on, Meg." Seth flashed her his boyish grin as he began to roll a ball of snow for their snowman.

Shoving aside her tumultuous thoughts, she decided her decision could wait for another day. It was Christmas, and the world was a beautiful blanket of snow, and her husband and son were waiting for her.

It took them quite a while to roll the first ball for the base of their snowman. Seth kept pelting Meghan with snowballs, making her squeal and race around the yard to dodge the cold bombs.

She managed to retaliate by shoving a handful of snow down his back. Kirk watched his parents in amusement, clapping his hands and laughing heartily at their antics.

They finished the base ball of snow and were working on the center one when Rose stuck her head out her front door.

"Merry Christmas to you all," she yelled.

"Merry Christmas, Rose," Seth and Meghan returned the greeting.

"Looks like fun," Rose exclaimed.

Seth grinned. "Pull on a coat and join us."

"Oh my, no!" Rose laughed. "I'm far too old for such nonsense. But when you get finished there, I've got hot coffee and freshly baked cinnamon rolls waiting for you."

"Sounds great," Seth replied.

Meghan waved and wondered if someday she would be like Rose. Would she end up all alone in the world, depending on the company of neighbors to keep loneliness at bay? Seth would be gone soon, and eventually Kirk would grow up and build his own life and family.

Would there be love after Seth? At the moment she couldn't imagine loving anyone as much as she did her ex-husband. The idea of being with somebody else, making love to another man, was positively distasteful.

"Are you okay?" Seth asked, obviously realizing she'd grown quiet. He set the center ball of snow atop the base ball, then brushed snow from her cheek and studied her intently.

"I'm fine." She flashed him a reassuring smile,

then added, "I'm just getting a little cold." It wasn't the temperature that was making her cold, it was her thoughts of life without Seth.

They finished the snowman, their laughter filling the air. They placed Seth's hat on his head, Meghan's scarf around his neck, then Meghan ran inside and got a carrot, a handful of red grapes, and a small orange halved. Seth helped Kirk make the face with orange eyes, the carrot nose and an oversized mouth of grapes.

"It's an awesome snowman," Meghan pronounced as they stepped back to admire their work.

"It is, isn't it?" Seth agreed.

"No man," Kirk said, then clapped his hands together with excitement.

Meghan laughed. "If he were older, we'd never get away with this."

"Get away with what?" Seth asked curiously.

"Playing in the snow and building a snowman before opening presents."

Seth looked at her in mock outrage. "Are you saying eventually my son will grow into one of those hedonistic little gift grubbers who awakens before dawn to see what sort of haul Santa left?"

"If he's normal, that's exactly what he'll become," Meghan said with another laugh.

"Are you ready for a quick cup of coffee with Rose?" Seth asked as he picked Kirk up in his arms.

"Sure," she agreed, knowing the day would probably be difficult for the woman all alone.

They traipsed to Rose's door and she greeted them

by kissing them each warmly on the cheeks. "Come in, come in," she said.

As Seth and Meghan took off their outerwear, Rose took off Kirk's snowsuit. "I see his chicken pox are scabbing nicely," she said. "You're lucky he had such a mild case."

"He should be able to go back to day care soon," Meghan said as they followed Rose into the kitchen.

"No point in paying for day care as long as I'm here," Seth replied.

Meghan didn't reply. In truth, she wasn't sure how to reply. On the one hand, she knew he was right. There was no point in taking Kirk to day care while he was home to care take for Kirk.

And yet, she felt the need to get things back to normal. Seth was not a permanent fixture, and they were being foolish in pretending that he was.

Rose gestured them to the table and placed Kirk on the floor in front of her pots and pans cabinet. "What a perfect Christmas day," she said as she poured them each a cup of coffee. "Nothing like a Christmas Eve snowfall to make everything seem right with the world."

"It is beautiful, isn't it?" Meghan said, looking out the window to Rose's backyard.

"Of course, you both realize men all over the city are cussing the snow, knowing before the day is out they'll be outside shoveling the stuff," Seth said.

"And if one man was really nice, he'd shovel off my walk before the day is out," Rose said with a sly grin.

Seth looked pained. "I knew there was a price to pay for freshly baked cinnamon rolls."

Rose laughed and placed the platter of the sweets in the center of the table. "Help yourselves," she said, then sat down with them.

Meghan took a bite of one of the sticky rolls. "Oh, Rose. These are delicious," she exclaimed.

Rose smiled in satisfaction. "Thank you, dear. It was my mother's recipe." She took a sip of her coffee and eyed first Seth, then Meghan. "I finally figured it out," she said.

Meghan frowned in confusion. "Figured what out?"

"About you and Steve."

Seth grinned at Meghan. "She absolutely refuses to believe we're cousins."

"If you're cousins, then I'm Peter Pan," Rose exclaimed. "And you aren't about to see me wearing a pair of green tights and flying around the air." She paused a moment, then continued. "I know you're lovers, I just can't figure out why you are trying to keep it a secret."

Rose directed her gaze at Meghan. "Maybe it's because you thought I'd think less of you because you and Steve aren't married?"

She didn't wait for Meghan's reply. "I might be old, but I know things are different nowadays, and I'd only think less of you if you weren't sleeping with a hunk like Steve here."

Meghan wasn't sure whose face was more red, hers or Seth's. "Okay, you found us out," Seth said.

"We're lovers, but Meghan was afraid you'd think she was a loose woman."

"I knew it!" Rose slapped the table and cackled with glee. "So, when are you going to marry her and make an honest woman of her?"

"I have no interest in marrying Steve," Meghan said hurriedly, then felt her blush intensify.

"I'm good enough to sleep with, but not good enough to marry?" Seth looked at her in mock disappointment, his eyes glittering with amusement.

"I don't think I'd let him get away, Meghan," Rose added. "He's definitely a keeper."

A keeper who didn't want to be kept, Meghan thought with a touch of bitterness. She was grateful when the topic of conversation changed from her and Seth's relationship to the forecast for more snow.

By the time they had finished talking about the weather, Meghan and Seth were ready to head back home. They redressed in their coats and gloves, wishing Rose a very merry Christmas.

"Wait," Rose said before they could get out the door. She disappeared back into the kitchen, then returned with three presents. "It isn't much," she said as she handed them all to Seth.

"Rose, you shouldn't have," Meghan protested.

"Oh hush," Rose admonished. "It's just a little something for each of you. Now go on, get out of here and enjoy the rest of the day."

Once back at Meghan's, Seth plugged in the Christmas tree and built a fire in the fireplace while Meghan changed Kirk. Then, together they sat on the floor in front of the tree to watch Kirk open his Christmas presents.

Meghan helped him with the wrapping paper, which seemed to intrigue him far more than whatever was inside. It took most of the morning to get through all the presents and by the time he played a little with each one, his eyes were drooping with the need for a nap.

"Why don't you go feed him some lunch and put him down, and I'll take care of the cleanup in here," Seth offered.

"Okay," she agreed. As she picked up Kirk and carried him into the kitchen, Seth had already begun stuffing the discarded boxes and bright-colored paper into a garbage bag.

Thirty minutes later, she left the nursery and went back into the living room. The room was picked up, the fire crackled merrily and Seth sat on the sofa, staring into the flames.

He smiled at her as she walked in. "He asleep?"

"Almost before I put him in the bed. Between the time outside playing and the excitement of new toys, he was exhausted."

He patted the space next to him. "Come and sit with me for a minute."

She sat next to him, fighting the urge to lean against him, close her eyes and pretend that they would have a happy ending.

He put his arm around her shoulder and she gave into half her urge and leaned against him. "There's nothing better than a fire on a snowy day,'' he said softly.

"It is nice, isn't it," she agreed. "Last year I don't think I made a fire more than twice during the whole winter."

"How come?"

She shrugged. "I don't know. It seemed like a lot of work for just me to enjoy a fire."

"I thought maybe you made a fire and sat like this with baldy."

Meghan sat up and stared at Seth. "Baldy?"

His cheeks flushed a dull red. "David."

Meghan relaxed against him, her gaze focused once again on the fire. "I called David the other day and told him I wouldn't be seeing him again... although we never really started seeing one another. There were just no sparks, nothing happening with him for me."

"I'm sorry," he replied.

"Don't lie. You aren't a bit sorry. You didn't like him."

He didn't bother to deny her words. "Should we open our presents from Rose?"

"Okay," Meghan agreed. Seth picked up the two gifts from the floor. Kirk had opened his earlier, a toy phone that he'd chattered in for several minutes before moving to the next new toy. "You first," Meghan said.

Seth unwrapped the small package to find a key chain with half a large red heart dangling from the chain. "I'll bet I can guess what yours is," he said.

Meghan unwrapped hers to find a key chain with the other half of the heart. "Rose is nothing if not a romantic at heart," she murmured.

"She's a nice woman, even if she is incredibly nosy," Seth said. "I got you something, too." He leaned over the edge of the sofa and pulled out a large, beautifully wrapped package.

"Oh, Seth. You shouldn't have," she protested. "I...I didn't get you anything." She'd considered buying him something, but had finally decided against it.

"You've opened your house to me. You've allowed me to share the holidays with you and my son. I'd say you've given me a wonderful present."

His words caused tears to spring to Meghan's eyes. She quickly averted her gaze to the gift in her lap. Carefully, she untied the huge gold bow and unfastened the tape that held the gold and scarlet paper together.

"You are the most irritatingly patient gift unwrapper," Seth said in bemusement. "Most people just tear the hell out of the paper."

"Half the fun of a gift is the anticipation of revealing it," she countered.

She unwrapped the box and neatly folded the paper and laid it to the side. Lifting the top of the box, she gasped as the content was revealed.

It was a nightgown. Not just any gown, but a glorious white silk, with tiny seed-button decorations and lacy insets across the bodice.

"I remember on our wedding night you were all

upset because things had happened so fast and you didn't get a chance to buy a nightgown fit for a bride.''

His words, coupled with the unexpected gift, brought on deep emotion that choked her with intensity.

''Excuse me,'' she mumbled. Still clutching the gown, she ran to her bedroom, needing some privacy.

She sat on the foot of her bed and allowed the tears that had choked in her throat to escape. They seeped hot and abundant from her eyes and slid down her cheeks.

The fact that Seth had remembered her wish for a pretty nightgown on her wedding night amazed her. The fact that he'd attempted to fulfill that wish, even though it was far too late, touched her beyond measure.

She swiped at her tears and gazed down at the nightgown in her lap. They had married in haste... driven by an incredible need for one another. There had been no time for wedding finery or planning an unforgettable wedding night. However, their wedding night had been memorable despite the lack of planning and forethought.

The silk felt cool and luxurious against her hands and suddenly she wanted it on, skimming her body.

Undressing, she knew exactly what she intended. She wanted the wedding night with Seth now...in the middle of Christmas day while Kirk napped.

Her desire for Seth had simmered for the past

week and now it was on the verge of an explosion. She intended to let it explode.

She undressed quickly, her hands trembling slightly with anticipation. She pulled the gown over her head and let it fall against her curves like a cool waterfall of silk.

Turning around, she faced her reflection in the dresser mirror. It fit beautifully. Seth had always been good at buying the correct size for her. The rounded neckline tastefully exposed the swell of her breasts without being overt, and the tapered waist made her appear willow slender.

A fairy princess. She felt like a fairy princess waiting for her prince to join her in the marital bed. Seth. Her prince…her love.

She took off her glasses and placed them on the nightstand, then opened her bedroom door.

He stood there, as if waiting only for her to call his name. For a long moment their gazes locked and held. His eyes called to her, saying everything that was in her own heart. He held out his hand and she drew him into her room and closed the door behind her.

"You look so beautiful," he said, his voice deep and husky as desire shone from his eyes.

"The gown is beautiful," she replied, still holding his hand.

"No," he countered. "You're beautiful. You've always been able to take my breath away, and nothing has changed. You still take my breath away." He leaned forward and gently touched his lips to hers.

They remained apart, not touching anywhere except for their lips. But Meghan felt the kiss sizzling through her entire body, as if he were intimately pressed against her.

Then his hands touched her shoulders, caressed across her back, and suddenly she was pressed intimately into him and he deepened the kiss by swirling his tongue against hers.

He broke the kiss and trailed his mouth across her jawline. "Meghan...sweet Meghan..." he whispered against her ear. "I want you. I've wanted you every moment of every day for the past week."

"As I've wanted you," she replied breathlessly. She tugged at the bottom of his sweater, indicating she wanted it off.

He stepped away from her long enough to pull the sweater off over his head and toss it to the floor. When he embraced her again, her hands splayed across his warm back, loving the play of muscles against her fingers and palms.

As his lips found hers again, Meghan realized the love she felt for Seth at this moment in time was different, far more profound than what she'd felt in the seven months they had been married.

When they'd been married, she'd been overwhelmed by Seth's lust for her, awed by the fact that this intensely handsome, slightly dangerous, highly sexual male was in love with her.

Now, she still felt all those things, but there were additional emotions that played into the whole package. Things like the way Seth's face lit up when he looked at Kirk, things like the patience he exhibited with his son. Seth as a man left her breathless. Seth as a man and a father had taken utter possession of her heart and soul.

She gasped as without warning he scooped her up in his arms. His gaze burned into hers, speaking volumes of the passion that flamed inside him.

He carried her to the bed and gently laid her down, then, gaze still locked with hers, he tore off his jeans and stretched out beside her.

For a long moment he made no move to touch her, caressing her only with a sweeping gaze that licked tongues of fire along her veins.

Meghan did the same to him, first holding eye contact with him, then moving her gaze to the breadth of his shoulders and across the dark hairs that gave his chest an erotic, masculine appeal. His stomach was lean, without an ounce of spare flesh. Heat washed over her as she stared at his arousal.

''If you keep looking at me like that, we're going to be finished here before we really get started,'' he warned.

She laughed, thrilled that she could affect him by a mere look. Her laughter stopped abruptly as he once again claimed her lips in a fiery kiss that drove all other thoughts out of her head.

The gown that had begun the whole scene was quickly discarded, tossed to the floor along with Seth's jeans, leaving her naked and vulnerable to his every touch.

His mouth was hot, hungry and demanding, and

he used it to love every inch of her body, filling her with an ache she feared might consume her. She thrashed beneath him, her hand grasping him, urging him to take possession of her. But he refused to hurry.

They made love slowly, languidly, as if they owned the hands of time and would not relinquish control until they absolutely had to. Each kiss called for another, every caress had a corresponding reply.

They spoke eloquently of their love, their desire for one another, without words, using only the universal language of touch.

When he finally entered her, Meghan was lost in a sea of sweet sensation, and Seth was her life raft. She clung to him, trapping him between her slender thighs, wanting to hold him there forever.

He slowly eased his hips back, until he was just barely inside her, then he moved forward, filling her up with his warm solidness. He repeated the motion several times, until she was crying out with pleasure.

"Meg…Meg…" His voice, a blend of a soft whisper filled with love and the tortured, naked need of a man for a woman, sent additional shivers through her.

He increased his pace…moving faster into her, his biceps muscles rigid as he worked his hips back and forth, sending her higher and higher on the crests of passion.

She cried out in surrender as wave after wave of pleasure crashed around her, inside her. And with a cry of his own, Seth relinquished his last grasp of control and surrendered to her.

Although Seth shifted his weight to her side, they remained entwined, neither in any hurry to break the sweetness of their intimacy.

A deep fulfillment, an utter contentment flooded through Meghan. She could feel Seth's heartbeat, strong and vital. The scent of him surrounded her, and she felt more safe, more secure than she'd ever felt in her life.

Closing her eyes, she sighed audibly. This was where she belonged, in his arms. And the utter contentment she felt at this moment enveloped her.

She wasn't sure, but she thought she might have fallen asleep for a few minutes. It was Seth's voice that pulled her from her half-sleep state.

"Meghan..." He trailed his hand across her bare back, as if loving the touch of her skin. "We need to talk."

His words caused a shiver of fear to race up her spine. She opened her eyes with a weary resignation, knowing the conversation they were about to have would irrevocably shatter the fantasy they'd been living the past week.

It was time for a reality check, and Meghan knew her heart was about to be broken all over again.

# Chapter 13

Meghan rolled away from Seth's embrace and grabbed her clothes. She didn't want to have this talk while naked and in his arms.

While she pulled on her clothes, Seth did the same, redressing in his jeans and sweater. "Let's go back in the living room to talk," he suggested, as if he didn't want to have the discussion in the room where they had just shared a beautiful intimacy.

Meghan agreed with a nod. She grabbed her glasses from the nightstand and followed him from the bedroom.

The last thing she wanted was to have this difficult conversation in the room where they had just made love. She knew if they remained in here she would be vulnerable to him, might agree to anything with the touch of him still imprinted on her skin.

When they went back into the living room, Seth placed several more logs on the fire, then stirred it with the poker to set them aflame.

Meghan curled up in one corner of the sofa, watching him work with the fire, her thoughts trying to untangle themselves. She was so conflicted about Seth, about if he should be a part of Kirk's life or not.

Things had been so clear to her when she'd first found out she was pregnant. Although she'd known it was the right thing to do to let Seth know he had a son, she'd been absolutely convinced that it was also the right thing to do to keep Seth out of their lives.

Seth finished with the fire and joined her on the sofa. His gaze was soft, tender as he looked at her. "Meghan..." he reached for her hand.

She pulled her hand from his, not wanting any contact with him as she desperately tried to decide what to do. Should she allow him to be an active participant in raising Kirk? As she thought of her own childhood, her heart rebelled against the very thought. "Seth, I'm just not ready to make a final decision where Kirk and you are concerned."

He took her hand again, this time refusing to allow her to pull away. "I don't want to talk about Kirk. We need to talk about us."

Meghan looked at him in surprise. "About us?"

"Meghan, I love you. I never stopped loving you." His voice was deeper than usual and intensity gave it a slightly shaky tone. His gaze burned into hers. "And I know you still love me."

"I do," she confessed, deep emotion rising inside her. "I never stopped loving you, Seth. I tried, I really did, but I couldn't."

He squeezed her hand tightly. "Then what in the hell are we doing to one another?" He released her hand and stood suddenly. "What in the hell are we doing pretending it's all about Kirk, when it's all about us?"

"Because there's no answer for us." The joyous emotion that had filled her at his words of love transformed to agony as she remembered the reasons they had parted, the reasons that would still keep them apart.

"There has to be an answer." Seth paced in front of the fireplace, his body taut with tension, a deep frown etched into his forehead. "We're two rational, adult people who love one another. Surely we can work out any kinks so that we can be together for the rest of our lives."

He stopped pacing and stared at her, his gaze filled with a combination of love and a hint of suppressed anger. "Dammit, Meghan. I don't just want to be Kirk's father. I want to be your lover, your husband, your future."

"Then quit your job."

The words tore painfully from her throat and hung in the air, suspended by tension. He continued to hold her gaze and she saw the anger rising, stirring the green of his eyes into turbulent seas.

"And it's that simple," he said, a touch of bitterness sharpening his tone. His hands balled into fists at his sides. "When you met me, I was a field agent. When we started dating, I was a field agent. And when you married me, I was a field agent. I have never understood when, exactly, my job became an issue." His voice rose angrily.

Meghan held his gaze, refusing to be intimidated by his anger. "It was always an issue. I told you when I first met you that I didn't date field agents."

"But you did date me. You slept with me. You fell in love with me...and I fell in love with you. We got married and you never mentioned anything about me quitting my job."

"I just thought you understood that's what I wanted." She felt the same helpless, hopeless feeling that she had almost two years before, when they'd had a discussion much like this one.

He drew in a deep breath, as if to steady himself. "Meghan, I don't understand the sacrifice you're asking me to make. I've never understood it."

Meghan pulled off her glasses and rubbed her forehead, then put her glasses back on. "That's because we never really talked. In all the time we dated, in all the time we were married, we never really talked about what was important to each of us."

"Then talk to me now." He rejoined her on the sofa and once again reached for her hand.

Meghan chewed her bottom lip thoughtfully. She'd never told Seth about her fear...never really explained to him about her childhood. Maybe if she'd told him years ago, he would have abided by her wishes and quit. Maybe if she'd told him they would have never divorced.

"Meghan...you said the other day that we were nothing more than intimate strangers when we married. Looking back, I realize you were right. We didn't talk enough. We didn't share enough. But that doesn't mean it's too late now."

His words gave her courage, the courage to go back in time and face her dismal childhood, attempt to explain to him why she refused to live her mother's life and make Kirk live her childhood all over again.

"You know my father was a cop," she began.

"Yeah. But what does that have to do with us?"

"Everything." Once again she extricated her hand from him. This time she stood, unable to sit, needing the physical activity of pacing while she talked about how the past colored the present.

"I told you how much my mother hated the holidays, especially Christmas because she was so afraid for my father." She stood in front of the fireplace and stared into the flames, her back to Seth. "What I didn't tell you is that she was afraid every night my father left for work."

Meghan closed her eyes, allowing herself to go back in time. "That fear filled our house every night. She'd cry, she'd wring her hands, she'd conjure up all kinds of horrible scenarios. It was a terrible thing to see, a terrible thing to feel."

She jumped as Seth's hands touched her shoulders.

He turned her around to face him. "Why haven't you ever told me about this before now?"

A blush stole across her face, warming her from the inside out. "I was ashamed and embarrassed." She stepped around him, dislodging his hands from her shoulders. "Oh Seth, you're so brave and so strong. I didn't want you to laugh at me."

She faced him again, the heat of her face intensifying as her blush deepened. "Why do you think I have to have night-lights burning all over the house? It's because some of that fear of my childhood is still with me."

"I wouldn't have laughed at you," he protested softly.

"It doesn't matter now." She threaded a hand through her hair, her thoughts still in the distant past. "My mom used to wake me up on the nights dad was at work. She'd be crying, telling me that if something happened to him, she'd die, too. I saw her torment, Seth. The utter terror that gripped her each time he walked out the door. I lived her torment and I won't do it again. I don't want that for myself, and I definitely don't want it for my son."

"Meghan, for God's sake, don't ask me to give up my work." His eyes held a tortured plea.

"I'm not asking you to give it up entirely," she protested. "You can still work for SPEAR. Just take a desk job, Seth. Get out of the field." She hadn't realized hope filled her heart until this very moment. But now, hope expanded inside her and she held her breath…hoping…praying he would give her the happily-ever-after she wanted with him.

His agony shone from his eyes. "Meghan, I would do anything for you…for Kirk, but I can't do this. Working for SPEAR as a field agent isn't just what I do…it's who I am."

"Then you aren't the man I can live with for the rest of my life." The hope she had momentarily entertained left her, making her feel weak and defeated and in pain. "It just proves what I've always known. What you feel for me isn't love, not really. If you truly loved me, you'd do this for me."

"If you truly loved me, you wouldn't ask me to do this for you," he countered with an edge of bitterness.

They were back at the same place they had been eighteen months before, when they'd bitterly said goodbye and parted ways.

"And now you understand why we can't build a life together. And you should also understand why I can't allow you to continue to be a part of Kirk's life."

She raised her chin defiantly as she saw the flames of rising anger igniting in his eyes. "I won't give him the kind of childhood I had. If we got remarried, if we tried to be together, Kirk and I would be afraid every time you left for an assignment. I won't have that for myself, and I won't have it for him."

"Now, let me tell you something," Seth said, advancing toward her. He stopped when he stood mere inches from her. "Your mother did a terrible thing to you."

Meghan gasped in surprise. "What are you talking about? This isn't about my mother...it's about your job."

"It wasn't about your father's job and it isn't about mine. It's about a grown woman infecting her child with fear."

He took her by the shoulders, as if he wanted to shake her until she agreed to whatever he wanted. "Your mother destroyed your childhood, not your father's job. I will have a relationship with my son, whether you like it or not."

Meghan jerked away from him, her own anger raising an ugly head. "I'm his mother, and I'll decide who he has a relationship with."

"And I'm his father, and nobody...not even you will keep him from me," he yelled. He drew a deep breath and raked a hand through his hair as if to steady himself.

"Any time I walk out that door, whether it's to go on an assignment or to get milk at the corner store, I'm at risk. I could be hit by a bus, or struck by lightning. Tragedies happen," he continued more calmly.

"But your job puts you at greater risk than if you were pushing papers at a desk," she countered unevenly.

"And how Kirk handles that is up to you. Kirk will take his emotional health from you. You can do one of two things. You can teach him to accept my job calmly, rationally, or you can do what your mother did to you and make him an emotional cripple for the rest of his life.''

Seth went to the hall closet and pulled out his coat. He put it on, then grabbed his stocking cap. "You can shove me out of your life, Meghan. But, you can't shove me out of Kirk's." With these final words, he left the house, slamming the door behind him.

Meghan stared at the fire, the dancing flames blurring as tears filled her eyes. Just as she'd anticipated, the fantasy had shattered.

There would be no happily-ever-after for herself and Seth. She refused to compromise on this particular issue. She'd watched her mother disintegrate beneath the burden of fear. She loved Seth desperately, devotedly...but she couldn't surrender on this particular point. She refused to spend her life with a man who could be killed at any moment.

As long as Seth worked as a field agent for SPEAR, their futures would be separate from one another, no matter how much they loved one another.

Seth stalked around to the back of the town house and opened the shed. Anger coursed through him as he grabbed a snow shovel, needing some physical work to ease the tension that rolled inside him.

He wasn't sure who his anger was directed at, Meghan, himself, or fate...who had given him and Meghan a taste of what could be if only one of them would give in.

He went back to the front of the house and began to shovel the sidewalk, his thoughts in turmoil. She'd never told him before about her childhood and the needy mother who had used a child as a sounding board for fear.

Scooping up a shovelful of snow, he realized that at least now he better understood Meghan's demand, although he still believed it was unreasonable.

However, it was more than reason that kept him from granting her what she wanted...demanded of him.

Every time he thought about quitting his job as a field agent, panic pressed suffocatingly tight in his chest. A dreadful sense of impending doom engulfed him and he knew, rational or not, that if he quit his job he would die.

It was a feeling he could share with nobody, a feeling of weakness that shamed him. He especially couldn't tell Meghan, who believed him to be brave and strong.

He'd told the truth when he said to Meghan that being a field agent wasn't just what he did. It was who he was and without it he'd be nothing.

And so in the end, they were right back where they had been almost two years ago...in love, but unable to make it work.

Not quite where they had been, he amended. He shoveled more snow, methodically moving down the walkway in front of the house. Kirk. His head filled with a vision of his son.

Smiling, drooling Kirk was the difference between

the past and the present. Never again would Seth be simply a divorced man. For the rest of his life he would be a father.

Seth knew what it was like to grow up without a father. His own father had been a dead man in a recliner for years before he'd tragically ended his own life. There had been no father-son bonding, no baseball games or fishing trips. In truth, there had been scant little interaction between Seth's father and Seth.

Things will be different with Kirk, Seth vowed as he finished the walkway in front of Meghan's house and moved to shovel the one in front of Rose's place.

He didn't give a damn what Meghan wanted. He didn't give a damn what she demanded as far as Kirk was concerned. No power in the world would keep Seth from being a father to his son. Meghan would just have to figure out how to deal with what Seth did for a living when it came to raising Kirk.

She'd made it quite clear she would not deal with what he did for a living where she was concerned. Bitterness ripped through him, a bitterness born of enormous pain and disappointment.

He hadn't realized how much he'd hoped they could work out the issue and build a life together until now, when all that hope had fled.

*Just quit your job,* a little voice whispered inside him. *That's all it would take to make things right. Quit your job and Meghan will be yours forever.*

He gasped, his breath exploding out of him in a huge puff of icy smoke. He couldn't quit his job. He couldn't explain it, didn't understand it, but he knew this was the one thing he couldn't do for her.

He sat down on a bank of snow, trying to catch his breath.

He wasn't sure if his breathlessness came from his physical exertion or the terror that always gripped him when he thought of quitting his job.

He drew deep breaths, the icy cold aching in his chest. Why couldn't she just accept him for what he was? She'd married him, vowed to love him forever, then had changed all the rules.

The fear inside him transformed to a renewed dose of bitterness. Why couldn't she understand that without his job, he was nothing, and if he was nothing, what did he have to offer her or Kirk?

He reached into his pocket and pulled out the key chain Rose had given him. She had no idea how appropriate the gift had been. He was a man with only half a heart.

With an ache of emptiness inside him, he picked up his shovel and got back to work.

"You have big plans for tonight?" Mark asked Meghan as the two prepared to go home after working on yet another Sunday.

"Tonight?" She looked at him blankly, then sighed as she realized the date. New Year's Eve. The time of new beginnings, resolutions and hope. "Sure, my big plans are to get into my pajamas and be in bed by ten."

"In bed alone?" Mark asked with a sly grin.

Meghan didn't return the grin. "Definitely." Her tone of voice obviously spoke volumes to how things stood between herself and Seth, as Mark asked no more questions.

Moments later in her car driving home, Meghan thought about the past six days. Since their heated discussion on Christmas Day, she and Seth had kept a wary distance between themselves.

They shared their evening meal together with Kirk, then separated for the rest of the night. She wasn't sure what Seth did in the evenings as she usually took Kirk and went into her office to work on the computer.

She did know Seth's restlessness had increased tenfold. It was as if when he'd thought he and Meghan might be able to work out their problems and build a life together, the demons inside him quieted. But now that he knew a future between them was impossible, he was tense and filled with agitation.

He was ready for a mission. Meghan knew the signs. Seth needed action, adventure and excitement. It was best that they had decided not to try again with each other. She'd never be enough for him. He'd eventually grow to resent her for making him give up his job.

She'd been a fool to marry him in the first place, a fool to believe they could ever make a real life together. She pulled into the driveway, dreading another night of isolation and silence.

She couldn't help but retain a bit of anger toward

him. She hadn't forgotten the hateful, hurtful things he'd said about her mother. He just didn't understand...and he never would. He hadn't lived her life, hadn't experienced her childhood.

Shutting off the car engine, she touched the half a heart on her key chain. Half a heart. That's what Seth would leave her when he moved on. He would always have possession of half of her heart.

Wearily she climbed out of the car and went into the house. Silence greeted her. The deep, profound silence that indicated a place void of people.

"Hello?" she called out as she hung her coat in the closet. She dropped her purse on the entryway table and walked through the living room to the kitchen.

"Seth?" The kitchen was empty. There were no signs of dinner preparations, no evidence that anyone had been in the kitchen for some time.

Fear edged its way into Meghan's heart. Surely Seth wouldn't...she didn't allow the thought to flourish in her head.

They're probably playing in Kirk's room, she told herself as she hurried out of the kitchen and raced down the hallway. "Seth? Kirk?" She heard a subdued panic in her voice, a panic that increased when there was no answering reply.

They were not in the nursery, nor were they in any of the other bedrooms. Meghan stumbled back into the living room and stood there, trembling as her thoughts raced in frightening directions.

Seth had told her nothing would keep him from

his son. Had he been so afraid that she wouldn't allow him to be a father that he'd taken Kirk? Seth was an expert at disappearing. If he wanted, he had the ability to make certain nobody ever found him again.

She whirled around as the front door opened. Relief flooded through her as Seth walked in. "Seth…thank God."

"What's wrong?" he asked.

"I…I couldn't find you or Kirk…and I thought maybe…" She broke off, realizing how foolish, how unfair to Seth she had been in what she'd been thinking.

"Jeez, Meghan," he said and shook his head. "How could you even think that I would do such a thing."

Heat swept over her face. "I'm sorry…I just panicked." She frowned. "Where is Kirk?"

"I just took him next door to Rose," Seth explained as he pulled her coat out of the closet. "Here, put this on."

"Why? What's going on?" she asked as she walked toward him.

"Rose is baby-sitting Kirk for the evening. It's New Year's Eve," he said as he helped her with her coat. "I'm taking you out to dinner tonight."

"Are you sure you should do that? You don't want anyone to know you're here, but if anyone sees us together they'll know."

"It doesn't matter anymore." He moved to stand in front of her and buttoned up her coat. "I'm giving it one final week. If we don't find the information I need in a week, then it's time for me to move on.''

He smiled, although the gesture held no warmth. "So you see, you have something to celebrate tonight. It's the beginning of the end of me in your life.''

He opened the front door to usher her out. Celebration? Meghan thought about his words. He couldn't be more wrong. How could she possibly consider the final shattering of her heart an event to be celebrated?

# Chapter 14

Seth drove the short distance to Italia Gardens, the restaurant where he and Meghan had once had their first date. It seemed appropriate to him that they return there for their final "date" together.

He'd given himself another week to come up with the information about Simon, but for the past six days, ever since their argument on Christmas Day, he'd fought the need to be away from Meghan.

Loving her...wanting her...had no place in his life anymore and he knew the only way to get her out of his mind, out of his heart, was to get as much physical distance from her as possible.

"I hope you're hungry," he said as he pulled into the already crowded parking lot.

"A little," she said softly, her gaze lingering on

the exterior of the restaurant. "Why here?" She turned and looked at him, her expression somber.

"Because I remember how much you used to love their cheese ravioli. This was always your favorite restaurant."

"It hasn't been my favorite for a long time," she replied as she unfastened her seat belt.

"Would you rather go someplace else?"

She shook her head. "No, this is fine." She opened her car door to get out but he stopped her by grabbing hold of her arm.

"Meghan, I don't know about you, but this past week has been one of the longest in my life. I'm tired of the tension. Can't we just have a nice dinner together?"

For a moment, he thought she might cry. Her eyes had that luminous, vulnerable look that caused his heart to ache in his chest. She drew in a deep, tremulous breath. "A nice dinner sounds good," she agreed. She pulled her arm from his hand and got out of the car.

Together they walked into the small, intimate restaurant. "I have reservations," Seth said to the hostess, who took his name and gestured for them to follow her.

She led them to the same table where Meghan and Seth had shared their first meal together. The table was situated in a corner, isolated and intimate. A squat candle sat in the center of the table, spilling a soft glow of light onto the red-checkered tablecloth.

After they were seated, the hostess handed them

each a menu, then left them alone. The moment she left, Seth heard the telltale sound of Meghan's high heels dropping to the floor.

He grinned as a memory shoved into his head. "You remember that first night we came here and you took off your shoes beneath the table?"

Her eyes widened and a grudging smile curved the corners of her lips. "I'll never forget it. It was the most embarrassing moment of my life."

Seth laughed. "It took you, me and the waiter twenty minutes to find your shoes." Somehow, Meghan's shoes had been accidentally kicked from table to table while he and Meghan had eaten that night. When they got ready to leave, they'd had to hunt for two red high heels that had finally been found near the front door.

"I wanted to die," she exclaimed, her eyes sparkling like gems in the candlelight. "I wanted so desperately to make a good impression on you and there I was in my stocking feet, hunting under every table for my errant shoes."

"I thought it was charming. I thought you were charming," he said softly.

Their conversation was interrupted by the appearance of their waitress. She took their orders, brought them each a glass of wine, then left them once again.

Meghan sipped her wine, her gaze curious. "What made you decide to just give it one more week?"

Seth shrugged, knowing exactly what she was talking about. "I just realized there has to be an end to it. When I first showed up at your place, finding

Simon was all I could think about." He twirled the stem of his wine glass between his two fingers. "Somehow, over the past two weeks, that particular obsession has waned."

"I'm glad, Seth. And I hope you don't still feel responsible for the L.A. sting going bad."

He sighed and took a sip of his wine. "I can't help but feel partially responsible, but I guess I realize now the chain of events that happened were not under my control."

To his surprise, Meghan reached across the table and took his hand in hers. "You shouldn't be haunted by events you can't control. You're a good man, Seth."

But not good enough for you to take me as I am. The sentiment sprang unbidden to his mind, and he consciously shoved it away. He didn't want any bitterness between them.

He turned his hand over, so now it was his that captured hers. Small and delicate, he thought he felt a slight trembling. He squeezed it and smiled at her. "Spending these last two weeks with you and Kirk put things into perspective for me. I still want to find Simon, but it's time to put the obsession aside and move on."

She nodded and pulled her hand from his. "It's time we both move on."

Again their conversation was interrupted by the waitress, who served them their salads and placed a basket of bread sticks on their table. For a few minutes they ate in silence.

Seth studied Meghan, somehow feeling as if this would be his last opportunity to memorize her features. The candlelight loved her features, accentuating her cheekbones, her full lips and her beautiful eyes. The flickering light made her freckles appear to dance across her skin, freckles Seth had always found sexy as hell.

"You're staring," she accused.

"I know." He averted his gaze to his salad.

"Seth?"

He looked back at her again.

"About Kirk…" She wiped her mouth with her napkin and shoved her salad plate aside. "I won't fight you if you want to continue to see him, be a part of his life."

Her words shocked Seth, who'd assumed they'd have to have another round of fighting on this particular subject.

"Don't look so shocked," she said dryly. "I'm a mother, not a monster."

"And you're a terrific mother," he agreed, his heart expanding as he realized she was overcoming her fear to allow him to have a relationship with his son. "I know this was a difficult decision for you."

She shrugged. "In the end, not so difficult after all." She paused as the waitress appeared to serve their entrées. When the waitress had once again left the table, Meghan continued. "Rose was right when she said every little boy needs his father in his life. I've watched you with Kirk since you've been here. You're a good father, Seth."

"Thank you," he said simply.

"Don't thank me," she protested. "I'm doing this for Kirk, not for you," she said, as if needing to make this point clear to him.

"It doesn't matter what your motivation is for agreeing, I'm just grateful we don't have to fight about this any longer."

Meghan smiled, and in her smile Seth saw a deep weariness. "I'm tired of fighting, Seth. I don't want to fight with you anymore, either."

He nodded. "It's important that we get along. Whether we like it or not, our lives and our futures are bound together by Kirk." He fought against the despair that threatened to engulf him as he thought of what their future would now be with one another.

He would see Meghan not as his wife, but merely as the mother of the son they both loved. It was likely that one day Meghan would fall in love again, eventually remarry. This thought brought a renewed burst of pain to pierce his heart.

At least he had Kirk. That's what he had to focus on. He would have the relationship with his son that his father never had with him.

Again silence fell between them as they focused on their meal. As Seth ate, he found himself remembering the hunger he'd felt as a child, the hunger for a touch, a kind word, a bonding moment with the man who was his father.

His father had been on his mind a lot. He'd had several nightmares in the past week, playing and replaying in his sleep the tragedy of his father's death.

"You've gotten terribly quiet," Meghan observed as she finished the last of her ravioli.

"Just thinking," he replied.

"About?"

"About the fact that when you said we were intimate strangers when we got married, you were right."

She raised an eyebrow. "What brought this on?"

He took one last bite of his lasagna then shoved his plate away. "Are you ready to go?"

"Okay," she said, her forehead wrinkled in bewilderment.

As Seth paid the bill, he wondered why he felt the sudden need to talk about his father. He'd never told anyone about that day...the birthday that had destroyed any hope of a relationship with the man he'd desperately needed in his life.

But for some reason he wanted to talk to Meghan. He wanted her to understand exactly why he intended to be the best damn father in the world to his son.

"What's going on, Seth?" Meghan asked when they were back in the car and driving back toward the house.

What was going on, indeed? Why the sudden need to bare his soul to a woman he was about to walk away from? He didn't stop to question his motivation, he just decided to follow his heart.

"I don't know," he finally confessed. "I was just sitting there eating and thinking about the fact that it had taken a divorce and a considerable amount of time for you to tell me about your childhood."

"We didn't talk enough before we got married, and we certainly didn't talk enough after we got married," she observed. She stared down at her hands in her lap. "If we'd talked, we would have known that our dreams, our expectations for our future were miles apart from one another."

"But we got one thing right. Kirk."

She smiled at him, a smile that held a bittersweet melancholy. "Yes, we got that right."

"I can't tell you how grateful I am that you're not going to fight me about being in Kirk's life. I want to be a good father to him. I intend to be the kind of father my old man never was to me."

As he turned the corner near her town house, he felt her gaze on him.

"What do you mean?" she asked.

Seth went past her house, realizing he wanted the physical activity of driving while he told her about his father. "I mean I lied to you when I told you my father died in a car accident."

"You lied?"

He nodded, tightening his grip on the steering wheel. "My mother really did die in a car accident when I was twenty. My father committed suicide on my seventeenth birthday, but for all intents and purposes he was already dead for most of my childhood."

Shock riveted through Meghan at his words. "Oh my God, Seth." For a moment she was speechless. Suddenly she remembered the night he'd had his nightmare, the night she'd thought she'd heard him cry out the word "dad." "Seth, why didn't you tell me this before?"

He chuckled, a dry, hoarse sound that had held no mirth at all. "Probably for the same reasons you didn't tell me about your childhood of fear. I was embarrassed and ashamed. Thinking about it made me feel angry and weak and afraid."

He clutched the steering wheel so tightly his hands were white, the veins corded with tension.

"Pull over," Meghan demanded.

He shot her a look of surprise. "Why?"

"Just park the car."

He pulled to the curb and put the car in park. "What's going on?"

"This." She unbuckled her seat belt and scooted over and wrapped her arms around him.

It was sheer love that drove her, even knowing that he was leaving, even knowing that they could never be truly together. It was sheer love that made her need to hold him.

"Oh, Seth...Seth," Meghan crooned, stroking his hair as she held him close. "What an awful, horrible thing for you."

He leaned his head into the crook of her neck and she felt the tension that still vibrated in his body. In all the time she'd known Seth, loved Seth, she'd never felt him need her as he did at this moment.

"Talk to me, Seth," she whispered in his ear, knowing the only way to exorcise demons was to expose them to the light. "Tell me about your father."

He pulled away from her embrace and slumped back in his seat, his gaze directed out the car front window where the illumination of streetlamps transformed the lingering snow into a frosting of icy crystals.

Meghan sat back in her seat, patient as she watched the myriad emotions flirt across Seth's features. Pain...shame...torment...they were all there and she reached over and grabbed his hand in an effort to give him strength.

He squeezed her hand, as if reassured by its very presence in his. He drew a deep breath. "I loved my old man. When I was really young, I thought he was the strongest, biggest man in the world."

She smiled. "I'm sure that's exactly what Kirk thinks of you."

Turning to look at her, his eyes flashed with bright gratitude. "Dad worked until I was about eight. I don't know exactly what he did...sold insurance, I think. But, about the time I was eight, he quit going to work on a regular basis and started spending a lot of time sitting in his chair and staring at the television. About that time Mom starting working two jobs. I realize now it was probably because of financial problems."

"But I'm sure it felt like a double abandonment," Meghan replied.

His eyes lit up in surprise at her words. "Yeah, I guess it did. The father I knew disappeared and Mom was never home. Anyway, as time went on, Dad got worse and worse. He spent all his time in his chair wrapped in an afghan. He rarely spoke, never laughed and seemed to live solely in his own mind.''

Meghan squeezed his hand. "It sounds like your father was ill."

"I realized that as I got older," he agreed.

"Did he see a doctor?"

"Yeah, about once a month Mom would take him to a psychiatrist who prescribed medication, but I never really saw any improvement in him."

Meghan felt the tension inside him growing. It was a palpable force that radiated like a living entity.

Again his hands sought the steering wheel, as if he needed to hang on as he went back into the darkness of his past. "That day...my seventeenth birthday, I came home from school and found that my dad had taken his revolver and killed himself." Meghan wanted to reach for him again, but something in the tilt of his head, the rigidity of his body indicated he didn't want to be touched at the moment.

"I...I smelled the gun powder as soon as I walked into the house. When I went into the living room and saw him slumped in his chair all I could think about was that the bastard had gone and ruined my birthday." Seth turned haunted eyes to Meghan. "Isn't that horrible? My father had just shot himself to death and I was pissed because he'd ruined my birthday."

Meghan saw the unshed tears in his eyes, glazing

the green depths, but refusing to give way. She recognized his enormous guilt and pain and the strength it took to hold those emotions inside.

"Seth, you were a boy," she said softly. "And I'm sure it was easier to manage anger than it was to manage the incredible hurt you felt."

He closed his eyes, cords of muscles taut in his neck. She saw him swallow once…twice and knew he was desperately fighting for control. She averted her gaze from him, knowing his pride would never allow him to cry in front of her.

"I couldn't understand why I wasn't enough for him," Seth said after several minutes had passed. "I couldn't understand why he hadn't wanted to live for me."

Meghan could stand it no longer. Once again she reached for him and wrapped him in her embrace. "He was sick, Seth. I'm sure it had nothing whatsoever to do with you. He was sick and in mental pain and sometimes that pain is so great nothing can ease it."

He shuddered in her arms. "As a man, I know that. As a boy, I didn't understand, couldn't understand. All I know for certain is that I want to be there for Kirk. I don't want him to grow up with the same kind of hunger that I felt."

He remained in her arms for a long time. She stroked his hair, grieving for the fatherless boy, the young man who had found the body of a father who had given up on life.

He finally pulled away from her and gave a shaky

laugh. "We'd better get home." Meghan nodded, knowing he would probably never again speak of his father's death.

Hopefully telling her had been enough to drive away whatever nightmares haunted him, to ease the infection of festering wounds.

It was almost nine o'clock when they got back home. Seth went next door to get Kirk and Meghan booted up her computer to check her e-mail.

She initiated the powerful search engine she'd programmed to hunt for new articles that concerned any recent influx of drugs, busts and seizures, then leaned back in her chair and watched as the machine did its thing.

She tried to run the engine every night so that each day she received a new listing of drug related articles from newspapers around the country. A half a dozen new ones showed on her screen. Quickly, she scanned each one, dismissing them one by one as she realized they didn't contain the information Seth sought.

However, when she got to the fourth news article, her heart skipped a beat. It was a small report translated from a Spanish newspaper. It indicated that an unidentifiable source stated that a huge shipment of heroin had entered the country and law enforcement had stepped up their efforts to find the cache and arrest the guilty.

The news clipping was from the tiny republic of Madrileño, Central America. She hit the button to print the note. As it printed, she stared at the screen, knowing this was the information Seth had been waiting for. This was the information that would take him finally, irrevocably away from her.

Just shut off the computer, a little voice whispered in the back of her head. Shut it off and pretend you never turned it on tonight.

And then what? Hide it for a day…a week? She already knew she and Seth were lost to one another, so why put off the final parting?

Seth appeared in the doorway, a sleeping Kirk in his arms. "I'm going to put him in bed," he said.

She nodded absently as he disappeared from the door. He returned a moment later. "What are you doing?"

"I just stopped in here to check my e-mail."

"Anything interesting?"

She hesitated, wanting to say no…wanting to turn the computer off and love Seth enough that he'd forget his job, forget his duty.

"Yes." She picked up the paper from the printer and handed it to him.

She watched his face as he scanned it, saw the energy that suddenly possessed him, the dangerous glint that usurped all the lightness from his eyes. "It's him, isn't it?"

"There's no way to be certain, but I would say it's highly probable."

He gripped the paper tightly in his hand. "I'm going to the kitchen to use the phone."

Before she could even nod, he was gone. Meghan shut down the computer, her heart aching. She'd thought she'd prepared for this moment, believed she was ready to tell Seth goodbye. She'd been wrong. There was no way to prepare for heartbreak.

All you have to do is give in. The words filled her mind as she shut off the office light. She could make it all right by telling Seth she loved him and didn't care if he continued working as a SPEAR operative. All she had to do was sacrifice all that she'd believed in, wished for and she and Seth could be together.

She thought of those nights when her father had gone to work, nights of fear and anguish. Did she want to live a life like that?

No, she couldn't.

Eventually her fear would destroy their marriage. Seth would grow tired of her fear, they'd begin to resent one another and eventually she'd be alone again anyway.

She walked out of the room and was met by Seth in the hallway. "It's done," he said.

She fought the impulse to reach up and shove a strand of his unruly long hair from his forehead, knowing that in a single touch she might lose control and weep. "When do you go?"

"First thing in the morning." He looked as alive, as vital as she'd ever seen him. "Meghan, I know I've already asked too much of you, but I have one more request."

"What?"

"Tonight." His gaze burned into hers. "Tomorrow I'll be out of your house, out of your life except for visits with Kirk. Give me tonight with you in my arms. Give us one more night together before I leave.''

She wanted to tell him no, that he was asking too much, taking too much. But she had no defenses where he was concerned. Tomorrow he'd be gone. They only had tonight. One last night of loving Seth before a lifetime of grief and loneliness.

He opened his arms to her and despite the fact she knew it was another mistake in a long list of mistakes where he was concerned, she went into his arms.

# Chapter 15

Meghan awakened just before dawn, knowing before she even opened her eyes that Seth was gone. She stretched a hand out across the bed and felt the cold emptiness where there had been warmth and life and love.

"Happy New Year," she said aloud, fighting back tears. Those had been the last words Seth had said to her, after making love to her with a ferocity that had overwhelmed her.

Her body still ached from his lovemaking, but that ache had nothing on the one that lived in her heart.

She pulled herself out of bed, checked to make sure Kirk was still sleeping soundly, then stumbled into the kitchen to make coffee.

The silence of the house had never been so deep,

had never been so profound. And she had never felt so hopelessly alone.

She stared at the coffee dripping into the carafe, her heart aching as it had never hurt before. Seth's smell lingered on her, as did the warmth of his caresses from the night before.

She suddenly felt the need for a shower. She needed to wash away the feel of his hands, the scent of him that haunted her. Checking again on Kirk, who still slept soundly, Meghan went into the bathroom for a long, hot shower.

As she stood beneath the spray of water as hot as she could tolerate, she wished some of the heat of the water could penetrate to warm the cold bleakness of her heart. She scrubbed at her skin with strawberry-scented soap, knowing despite her efforts it would take a long time before Seth's scent would banish itself from her mind, from her heart.

After her shower, she dressed in jeans and a sweatshirt and returned to the kitchen where she poured herself another cup of coffee.

Kirk wailed from the bedroom, indicating he was awake and ready to begin a new day. At least Kirk had gained a father, she thought as she went to get her son.

Kirk had gained a father and she had lost the love of her life.

She had just fed Kirk breakfast and was nursing her last cup of coffee for the morning when the doorbell rang. She opened the door to see Rose, clad in one of her trademark dusters and an overcoat. She carried an electric casserole in front of her.

"Happy New Year," Rose exclaimed merrily as she breezed past Meghan and headed for the kitchen.

"Come on in," Meghan said dryly, closing the door and quickly following the older woman.

Rose greeted Kirk and set the casserole on the table. "Where's Steve?" she asked. "Don't tell me that man is still in bed?"

"No, he's not in bed. He's gone. And his name isn't Steve, it's Seth."

"I knew it!" Rose exclaimed triumphantly. "I had a feeling all along he was the handsome devil you'd been married to."

She moved the casserole from the table to the counter and plugged it in. "I hope he won't be gone long. These black-eyed peas are ready to eat any time. And everyone knows you have to eat black-eyed peas to bring you good luck in the new year." She turned and smiled at Meghan.

Meghan burst into tears.

"Oh dear. Come and sit down," Rose guided Meghan to one of the chairs at the table, patting her back until she was seated. Rose sat opposite her and waited a moment for Meghan to compose herself.

"Mama," Kirk said and offered her a tentative smile.

"It's okay, honey. Mama's fine." Meghan swiped at her tears, not wanting to upset her son. She got up and handed him several little plastic trucks, then returned to her seat at the table.

"Now, talk to me," Rose demanded. "You look like a woman who definitely needs to talk."

And Meghan did need to talk. She told Rose about her childhood, about her father's job and her mother's fear.

When she explained to Rose what had torn her and Seth's marriage apart almost two years earlier, she told her Seth worked as a consultant to a large firm who dealt with war-torn countries. It was Seth's cover for his real job.

"His work takes him around the world, in places where he is in imminent danger," she explained. "After we got married, I didn't want him doing that anymore. I wanted him to take a safe job that would keep him with me forever." Meghan sighed and swallowed the tears that filled the back of her throat. "I love him, but I can't live with him and live the same kind of fear I did when I was a child."

"And he refuses to quit his work," Rose observed.

Meghan nodded. "He loves what he does. But I realize now he was right about one thing. My mother did me a disservice. As the adult, she should have never burdened me with the weight of her fear. She should have never shared adult concerns with a child."

"Did your father know how frightened she was when he went to work?" Rose asked curiously.

Meghan frowned, thinking back in time. "I don't think so." Every morning her mother greeted her father at the front door and never said a word about the fear that had gripped her while he was gone.

Funny, Meghan had forgotten about those mornings when her father would arrive home and he and her mother would hug with the joy of love and reunion.

"And she never asked your father to quit his job."

Meghan looked at Rose in surprise. "No, I'm sure she didn't." Meghan knew in her heart that her mother had never asked her dad to quit his job. Even though she had been racked by fear each time he left for work, she'd never tried to take the job away from him. Instead, her mother had rejoiced every day when he returned.

Had Meghan been wrong to expect Seth to give up all that he was?

Rose reached across the table and patted Meghan's hand. "Oh, honey, I hope things work out for you and Seth. I saw the way that man looked at you. Hopefully the two of you will figure it all out. I've never seen two people who belong together like you and Seth."

Rose stood and pointed at the casserole. "Eat some of those peas. I'll come back and collect my pot later." With these final words, she whirled out of the kitchen and a moment later Meghan heard the sound of the front door closing as Rose left.

*The two of you will figure it all out.*

Rose's optimistic words echoed in her head. Meghan knew that wasn't going to happen. It was too late now. She'd let Seth slip away once again.

She had no idea when he might return. They hadn't discussed a routine visitation schedule and she knew with Seth's job a normal schedule would never work.

She knew what would probably happen was that he would occasionally just show up on her front porch, ready to see his son. And she would accommodate him as well as she could, because he loved Kirk, and Kirk loved him.

And Meghan loved him and whether they were married or not, she would always worry about him, wonder about him. She'd been foolish to think that if he quit his job, they could live happily ever after. She'd been foolish to believe that Seth could survive being less than what he was.

She'd allowed her childhood to rule her future instead of allowing her heart full rein. She wanted Seth now and forever, whether he was a SPEAR field agent or a garbage collector. And it broke her heart that this realization came too late.

Seth was gone…and she had no idea when she'd see him again. She had no idea if he'd survive the mission was now on. Tears suddenly blurred her vision, hot tears of immense regret.

She loved Seth and wanted him in her life without concessions. She'd take him however she could have him. She'd learn to deal with his job. The tears spilled down her cheeks as she realized what a stupid fool she'd been.

Seth had left here knowing there was no chance for the two of them. So there was no reason for him to return to her. By the time he finally came back to visit Kirk, he would have put her firmly out of his mind, moved on as they both had said they needed to. He'd no longer love her.

Too late.

She'd come to her senses too late.

The next twenty-four hours passed in agony for Meghan. She spent every moment that she could at her computer in her home office, checking all her sources, delving into places she shouldn't be in an effort to learn what had happened in Madrileño.

Nothing. No news to indicate anything had happened. What was going on? Was Simon in Madrileño? Was Seth there now? Had there been a raid? Was Seth all right?

The agony of not knowing kept her awake that night. She tossed and turned, praying for Seth's safety. Although she knew she'd blown any chance she had for Seth to be a permanent part of her life, she just needed to know that he was okay.

Her worry pulled her from her bed before dawn the next day. She stood at the kitchen window, staring out at the snow that had begun to fall. Had it only been a week ago that she and Seth and Kirk had played in the snow? Had it only been a week ago that Seth had given her a nightgown fit for a bride?

Had it only been a little over two weeks since she'd gotten out of her car and seen him on the front porch? A tiny flare of hope had filled her then, hope that maybe…just maybe…he was there because he needed her, loved her.

And he had...but now all hope was gone.

She poured herself a cup of coffee and went into her office to boot up her computer, hoping there would be some news of what might have happened in the little republic of Madrileño.

It was noon when she saw the first news release that indicated a huge drug bust had taken place. An unspecified amount of heroin had been taken into custody by the Madrileño military and all the responsible parties were also in custody.

"Yes," Meghan whispered, knowing the bust had been a SPEAR operation, but since for all intents and purposes SPEAR didn't exist, the local military would take responsibility.

She scanned the article quickly, but there was no information on how many might have been injured or killed in the operation.

Seth. Her heart cried his name over and over again, hoping, praying that he was all right. By evening, the reports of the huge drug bust made the U.S. world news. Still, details were far too sketchy to put Meghan's mind at ease.

That night, after putting Kirk to bed, she took a shirt from the spare room closet and put it on. The shirt, one of Seth's flannel ones, still retained the scent of him and she pulled it close around her as she snuggled on the sofa in front of a blazing fire.

In the flames of the fire she saw all that might have been had she come to her senses sooner. She saw Seth, green eyes shining with laughter...eyes darkened with desire. She saw him with Kirk, the intense fatherly love transforming Seth's features from handsome to utterly irresistible.

The doorbell rang and she knew it was probably Rose come to deliver more goodies. She had come over the night before bearing still-warm brownies, and had mentioned that she intended to bake some chocolate chip cookies today. It was as if the old woman thought sweets and chocolate might help ease Meghan's heartache.

Meghan pulled open the door to see Seth. His face was drawn with exhaustion, a shadow of whiskers darkening his chin, but his eyes burned with energy. "We have to talk," he said without preamble. He swept past her, bringing with him the scent of the cold.

Meghan closed the door, her heart singing with joy. He was okay. He was safe. But her joy was tempered with concern. Something was wrong. She'd seen the look in his eyes that spoke of trouble.

She followed him into the living room, gasping as he twirled around and grabbed her shoulders. "We got him." His voice radiated with success. "We got him and he's now in custody of the Madrileño military. Simon is finished."

"Seth, I'm so glad." She wanted to wrap her arms around him and tell him she didn't care what he did as long as he loved her, as long as they could live together, raise Kirk as a family. But the words refused to come as Seth stared at her, frightening her with the intensity of his gaze.

"What's wrong, Seth?" she finally asked. Maybe

the two days he'd been gone had been enough for him to realize he didn't really love her at all. Maybe he'd returned to tell her he'd made a mistake, wasn't cut out to be a father, would grant her initial wish and stay out of their lives forever.

"Sit down, Meghan." He guided her over to the sofa where she sank down into the cushions.

He walked over to the fireplace and added a log to the dying embers. He picked up the poker and stirred and poked until flames once again danced merrily. He returned the poker to the stand, but continued to stand before the blaze.

"I've had a lot of time to think since I left here," he began, his back to Meghan.

She closed her eyes, steeling herself, afraid he was about to speak words that would forever remove him from her life. She opened her eyes and looked at him, the rigid posture, the energy that wafted from him. Something was definitely on his mind.

*Too late,* a voice of dread whispered inside her. *You waited too long to tell him you love him enough to allow him to be what he needs to be.* "Seth…I've been doing a lot of thinking, too…"

He whirled around and held up a hand to stop her from speaking any further. "I've waited two long days to say this to you, I need to say it now."

She nodded…fear cascading over her like an icy waterfall.

"The day my father died, my mother commented that she should have never asked him to quit his job. She said my dad was never the same when he stopped being an FBI agent.'' He raked a hand through his shaggy hair and took a step toward her. ''I'd forgotten that, at least consciously. But unconsciously I think it's always been with me. Every time I thought of quitting my job, terror would overwhelm me.''

He took two steps to his left, then three to the right, his pacing irregular as torment played on his features. ''That panic was horrible. My chest would ache, my heart would pound, and I was certain if I quit I would die.''

''Oh, Seth, why didn't you tell me?'' Meghan eyed him beseechingly.

He stopped his pacing and looked at her, his eyes dark pools of emotion. ''How could I tell anyone that? I'm a SPEAR agent. I'm supposed to be brave and strong and courageous. How could I admit to an irrational, terrifying fear?''

He walked over and knelt in front of her. ''I was afraid that if I quit my job I'd end up like my father, that I'd eat the end of my gun like he had. And if that happened, what good could I be to you and Kirk?''

He took her hands in his and she felt a small trembling in his. ''But recognizing where that fear was coming from has freed me from it. I am not my father and I would never do to Kirk what he did to me. Meghan, I love you. I want you to be my wife again. I'm not afraid anymore. I'll quit my job if that's what it takes for us to be a family again. You and Kirk are the real important things to me.''

Meghan's heart expanded to fill her with warmth and joy. She squeezed Seth's hands and shook her head. "No, Seth, it would never work, not that way. You were born to be a SPEAR agent, and I can't...I won't take that away from you. The only way we can be a family is if you keep your job, but promise me you'll be extra careful out in the field so you always come home to me and your son."

His eyes flared wide with surprise and he stood, pulling her up and into his arms. "Are you sure?" He seemed to hold his breath as he waited for her to reply.

"I'm positive." She placed her hands on either side of his face, loving the feel of his scratchy whiskers against her palms. "I love you, Seth, and I realized these past two days that it doesn't matter whether we're together or not. Even if we are apart, I still love you. I still worried and I still prayed for your safe return."

She smiled as she felt his heartbeat quicken against her own. "I can either entertain the worry and fear and we won't be together, or I can take comfort in the knowledge that when you come home, we'll be together, loving each other for whatever time we have between missions. I fell in love with a SPEAR field operative, and I'd be happy to be married to a field operative."

She was unable to say another word as his lips captured hers in a kiss that stole her breath and sent desire shooting through her body.

"Oh, Meghan," he murmured as their fiery kiss

ended. "I thought it might be too late. I thought my stubbornness might have ruined things for us."

She pressed her body into his, reveling in the tightness of his arms around her. "And I was afraid of the same thing. I was so afraid I'd waited too late to realize I want you in my life any way I can get you."

He cupped her face with his hands. "You've got me, Meg. For today, for tomorrow…for always. Marry me, Meghan. Marry me and make me the happiest man on earth."

"I'll marry you on one condition…if you continue doing fieldwork." She gazed at him, loving the spring green of his eyes that promised warmth and life. "The man I love is a man who believes what he's fighting for, a man committed to a great cause, a man I can't imagine being…doing anything else. I love you, Seth."

Again he covered her lips with possession and in his kiss, Meghan tasted the sweet passion, the laughter, the very love of their future together.

He stiffened as the phone rang. "I'll get it," he said and released her to pick up the receiver of the phone on the end table.

Instantly his tension was back and his eyes glittered with the flow of energy. "Yeah…yeah…no." He spoke in monosyllables and Meghan recognized instinctively that he was speaking to somebody from SPEAR.

Her heart thudded anxiously. Had she gotten him back only to lose him again so quickly? They'd only had five minutes to cement their future together. She wanted more time.

He spoke into the receiver, so low Meghan couldn't hear his words, then he hung up. He shoved his hands in his pockets and gazed at her. "Simon escaped from the Madrileño military."

"Oh, no!" Meghan gasped.

"And he's taken a hostage, a SPEAR operative named Margarita Alfonsa de las Fuentes." He raked a hand through his hair. "Details are pretty sketchy at the moment. Jonah found out when he was flying to Madrileño. Now he's on his way back to headquarters."

"And you need to leave." She tried to keep her voice as emotionless as possible, even though her heart ached with the brevity of their time together.

"Yeah, I've got to leave." He walked back over to where she stood and pulled her into his embrace. She closed her eyes, burrowing deeper, closer against him. "But I'm not going to Madrileño," he said against her ear. "I told them this is one rescue mission they have to handle without me."

Meghan tilted her head back to look at him. "Then where are you going?" she asked.

That light…the flames of fire danced in his eyes, warming Meghan as if she'd swallowed the fire and it now resided inside her. "I'm due a little rest and relaxation and I'm going with my wife and my son on our honeymoon. I know a great resort in California that will be just perfect for a honeymoon."

"Seth…." She managed only to get his name out

before his mouth was on hers, shooting the flames of desire, the blaze of love, hotter and higher inside her.

As Meghan kissed Seth, she knew this time they were going to make it. Their first instincts had been right. They belonged together. They had gone from intimate strangers to soul mates and they were going to spend a lifetime together, raising their son amid laughter, and passion and love.

\* \* \* \* \*

*Be sure to watch for Carla Cassidy's
next heartwarming romance,*

**JUST ONE KISS**

*available in January
from Silhouette Romance.
And now, turn the page
for a sneak preview of*

**THE SPY WHO LOVED HIM**

*by Merline Lovelace,
the next exciting book in*

**A YEAR OF LOVING DANGEROUSLY,**

*available from Intimate Moments
next month!*

## Chapter 1

"**W**hy doesn't he marry *her!* The way she drapes herself all over him, any fool can see Anna would love Carlos to wrap her in silver gauze and shield her from every cold breeze that blows her way."

Muttering into her crystal champagne flute, Margarita Alfonsa de las Fuentes leaned silk-sheathed hips against a stone balustrade. Behind her, the city of San Rico, capital of Madrileño, spilled down steep, jungle-covered slopes into a sea awash in moonlight. In front of her, tall French doors thrown open to the balmy January night gave an unobstructed view of the glittering crowd gathered to welcome the new Australian ambassador to Madrileño. Dancers in flowing gowns and elegant tuxedos swirled and dipped across the State ballroom's shining parquet floor to the lively strains of the Blue Danube waltz.

One dancer in particular held Margarita's irritated attention. Her cousin, Anna. Tiny, beautiful Anna, with the melting brown eyes, thick black lashes, and tumbling masses of the blue-black hair most Madrileñans were born with. Slender as the swaying sugar plants that formed the basis of their country's economy, Anna moved with a feather-like grace that thoroughly annoyed her cousin. As Margarita knew all too well, delicate, seemingly fragile Anna possessed the face of an angel and the temper of a wasp. The twenty-year-old would make life miserable for everyone around her when things didn't go her way.

Not that her dancing partner would care about her temper. Or even notice it. If Carlos married Anna, he'd spoil her outrageously…then leave her to sit docile and pampered at home while he went about the important business of men. He wouldn't be around enough to notice her vile moods, which Anna would hide from him in any case like a proper little wife.

But Carlos didn't want to marry Anna. He'd decided on Margarita as his bride-to-be. He'd even obtained her father's consent to the match.

Gritting her teeth against an all-too-familiar frustration, she tossed her head and downed the last of the champagne as she watched Carlos. Carlos Caballero, Madrileño's Deputy Minister of Defense, was six feet plus of solid muscle, bronzed skin, glossy black hair, and calm self-confidence. Margarita had known him most of her life and had adamantly refused to marry him for the past year... despite her mother's fervent urging, her father's blustery demands, and the traitorous needles of desire that shot through her whenever Carlos turned his sexy onyx eyes in her direction.

The fact that he sprang from the same aristocratic roots she did, had racked up a chest full of medals during his military service, and was considered the brightest mind in the Ministry of Defense, didn't overcome the man's liabilities as a life partner in Margarita's mind. He was everything she didn't want in a husband. Conservative. Traditional. Overprotective.

It didn't matter that he also possessed a smile that made girls sigh and grown women walk into walls. Or that he moved with a pantherlike grace under his elegantly tailored tuxedo. Or even that Margarita's chest tightened whenever she imagined his lean, muscled body pinning hers to the sheets.

What mattered was that he shared the oppressive, antiquated view of marriage of so many Madrileñan men. She'd broken with her family once over their clamoring desire that she marry someone of their choosing. Fled to the United States for college and graduate school. Gotten involved with the top-secret SPEAR organization.

She'd come back to Madrileño three years ago, determined to help her country rise to the promise of the new millennium. Determined as well to eradicate the drug trade that had crippled its economy for

years. That's why she'd fought for her job with the
Ministry of Economics. Why she'd joined SPEAR
when she was approached as a graduate student. Why
she was determined to help them capture the traitor
who had a personal vendetta against the entire
SPEAR agency.

"You look especially beautiful in moonlight."

She turned, and the sight of Carlos in white tie and
black tux raised goose bumps on her bare shoulders
and arms.

How did he do it? She wondered irritably. How
could he look so devilishly handsome and so mad-
deningly complacent at the same time? How did he
manage to set her back up with a mere compliment?
She wasn't idiotic enough to wish he admired her for
her mind *instead* of her looks, but an occasional ac-
knowledgement of her intellect might have elevated
his standing in her eyes considerably.

"Thank you."

Her terse response lifted one of his brows. Stroll-
ing across the balcony, he joined her at the railing.
At five-seven, Margarita was considered tall for a
Madrileñan. Even so, she had to tilt her head to look
up into Carlos's chiseled features.

"I like you in red," he murmured. His gaze drifted
down her throat to the swell of her breasts. "What
there is of it."

"I'm so glad." Oozing syrupy sweetness, she
smoothed her palms over the flame-colored sheath
that plunged to a deep *V* in both front and back. "I
thought of you when I chose this gown."

"I'm sure you did. You take particular delight in taunting me, do you not, *querida?*"

The lazy half smile caused a distinct flutter in Margarita's chest. As much as she'd like to, she couldn't deny the man's impact on her. Carlos radiated masculinity. Smooth, controlled, extremely potent masculinity. Ignoring the treacherous skip in her pulse, she took issue with his casual endearment. "I don't suppose it would do any good to remind you that I am not now, nor will I ever be, your 'darling'?"

"No good at all," he replied easily. "Any more than it would do for me to remind you that 'ever' is a long time. I'm a patient man. *Very* patient..."

# a Year of Loving dangerously

If you missed the first 5 riveting,
romantic Intimate Moments stories
from *A Year of Loving Dangerously*,
here's a chance to order your copies today!

| | | | |
|---|---|---|---|
| #1016 | **MISSION: IRRESISTIBLE** by Sharon Sala | $4.50 U.S.☐ | $5.25 CAN.☐ |
| #1022 | **UNDERCOVER BRIDE** by Kylie Brant | $4.50 U.S.☐ | $5.25 CAN.☐ |
| #1028 | **NIGHT OF NO RETURN** by Eileen Wilks | $4.50 U.S.☐ | $5.25 CAN.☐ |
| #1034 | **HER SECRET WEAPON** by Beverly Barton | $4.50 U.S.☐ | $5.25 CAN.☐ |
| #1040 | **HERO AT LARGE** by Robyn Amos | $4.50 U.S.☐ | $5.25 CAN.☐ |

*(limited quantities available)*

| | |
|---|---|
| **TOTAL AMOUNT** | $ _____ |
| **POSTAGE & HANDLING** | |
| ($1.00 each book, 50¢ each additional book) | $ _____ |
| **APPLICABLE TAXES\*** | $ _____ |
| **TOTAL PAYABLE** | $ _____ |

(check or money order—please do not send cash)

To order, send the completed form, along with a check or money order for the total above, payable to **A YEAR OF LOVING DANGEROUSLY** to: **In the U.S.:** 3010 Walden Avenue, P.O. Box 9077, Buffalo, NY 14269-9077; **In Canada:** P.O. Box 636, Fort Erie, Ontario L2A 5X3.

Name: _____

Address: _____ City: _____

State/Prov.: _____ Zip/Postal Code: _____

Account # (if applicable): _____    075 CSAS

\*New York residents remit applicable sales taxes.
  Canadian residents remit applicable
  GST and provincial taxes.

*Silhouette*®

Visit Silhouette at www.eHarlequin.com                AYOLD-BL5

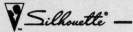

**Silhouette®**

# INTIMATE MOMENTS™

is proud to present a brand-new series
from *USA Today* bestselling author

# RUTH LANGAN

*The* **Sullivan Sisters**

**THE SULLIVAN SISTERS:**

LOVE IS A MOST UNEXPECTED GUEST FOR THREE
REMARKABLE SISTERS IN NEW HAMPSHIRE!

*Available only from Silhouette Intimate Moments
at your favorite retail outlet.*

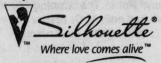

**Silhouette®**

*Where love comes alive™*

# INTIMATE MOMENTS™

presents a riveting 12-book continuity series:

*A Year of loving dangerously*

**Where passion rules and nothing is what it seems...**

When dishonor threatens a top-secret agency, the brave
men and women of SPEAR are prepared to risk it all as they
put their lives—and their hearts—on the line.

Available January 2001:

## THE SPY WHO LOVED HIM
### by Merline Lovelace

Although headstrong Margarita Alfonsa de las Fuentes was
mesmerized by Carlos Caballero's fearless courage, she wasn't
about to bow to *any* man. But now that a murderous traitor was hot
on their trail deep in the Central American jungle, the beautiful
secret spy struggled with the raw emotions Carlos's fierce
protectiveness stirred in her!

*Available only from Silhouette Intimate Moments
at your favorite retail outlet.*

## Silhouette®
*Where love comes alive*™

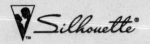